Gage wa

Except, he wasn't really back. He was just here to save her.

"All right," he said, and repeated it. "I need you to get on that plane and leave. I'll try to figure out who's after you and how to stop it."

That seemed like the goodbye she'd been expecting, and Lynette wanted to hang on to this moment just a little longer. "I could stay and help you."

"No deal." Another of Gage's sayings. In this case, he delivered it with a stubbornness that she had no trouble hearing.

Lynette opened her mouth to argue. She didn't want Gage shouldering all the danger. But then she thought of her unborn child. *Their* baby. If she stayed, the baby would also be in danger.

And that scenario was out of the question.

USA TODAY Bestselling Author

DELORES FOSSEN

GAGE

Recycling programs
for this product may
not exist in your area.

ISBN-13: 978-0-373-69632-1

GAGE

www.Harlequin.com

Printed in U.S.A.

ABOUT THE AUTHOR

Imagine a family tree that includes Texas cowboys, Choctaw and Cherokee Indians, a Louisiana pirate and a Scottish rebel who battled side by side with William Wallace. With ancestors like that, it's easy to understand why *USA TODAY* bestselling author and former air force captain Delores Fossen feels as if she were genetically predisposed to writing romances. Along the way to fulfilling her DNA destiny, Delores married an air force top gun who just happens to be of Viking descent. With all those romantic bases covered, she doesn't have to look too far for inspiration.

Books by Delores Fossen

CAST OF CHARACTERS

Gage Ryland—Ten years ago, he left Silver Creek after his marriage was annulled, but now he must "return from the dead" to protect his ex. He wants this to be a quick in and out, but he's not sure his heart will cooperate.

Lynette Herrington—Her domineering father forced her to end her marriage to Gage, and now she must come to terms not just with her past but her renewed feelings for Gage.

Ford Herrington—A powerful state senator and Lynette's father. In public, he's a respected, feared man. In private, he rules his family and business with an iron fist.

Patrick Harkin—Ford Herrington's business partner. He claims he's done nothing shady, but he could be lying.

Sampson Dalvetti—A drug lord with a vendetta against Gage. He's willing to use Lynette to get revenge.

Nicole Manning—She's Ford Herrington's longtime lover, and she could be afraid of what Lynette and Gage have learned about her.

Freddie Denton—A hit man hired to come after Lynette, but who sent him?

Chapter One

Gage.

Lynette Herrington's eyes flew open, and she jack-knifed to a sitting position in her bed.

Something had caused her to wake up.

But what?

With her breath gusting, her heart racing, Lynette glanced round her bedroom and then at the clock on the nightstand. Just past four in the morning.

Outside, a bad storm was playing havoc with the massive oaks on the side of her country house. The wind slapped at the branches, fanning them over the security lights mounted on the eaves. Rain slithered down the windows and made snaky shadows in the room.

"It's just the storm," she mumbled. That's what had pulled her from a deep sleep.

But something about that explanation didn't feel right.

She reached for the lamp switch, but the sound stopped her cold. It was hardly a sound at all, and the storm practically drowned it out, but Lynette was positive she heard something she didn't want to hear.

A single footstep.

"Don't scream," someone warned her. It was a man. And he was right next to her bed concealed in all those rainy shadows. "I won't hurt you."

Lynette's heart jumped to her throat, and she did exactly what he'd warned her not to do. She screamed. Or rather that's what she tried to do, but he muffled it by clamping his hand over her mouth.

"I said I won't hurt you," he repeated.

Lynette didn't believe him. She clawed at his hand and reached for the drawer of her nightstand where she kept a loaded .38. And by God, she knew how to use it. She wouldn't just let this man attack her or do heaven knows what else without her fighting back.

But the man fought back, too. He didn't let go of her, and whichever way Lynette turned and twisted to break free of him, he seemed to anticipate her every move. She couldn't reach the gun, and he was a lot stronger than she was.

Oh, God.

Was this how her life would end? With an intruder killing her in her own bed?

The fear of that caused her to freeze. But only for a moment. That's because she remembered she had a very big reason why she had to keep fighting. And why she had to win. She drew back her fist so she could punch him in the face.

"Gage sent me," the man growled.

It took her a moment to hear what he'd just told her. It was another moment before those words sank in. That was the only thing on earth he could have said to make her stop. Lynette quit struggling, and her gaze rifled to the man.

Gage.

Just the sound of his name put Lynette's heart in her throat again. It warmed her. And cut her to shreds all at the same time.

"Gage is dead," she whispered when he eased back his hand. "How could he have sent you?"

Unless…

Oh, mercy. She wanted to believe Gage was alive—especially since she'd never seen his dead body. Was that what this man was here to tell her? That Gage wasn't dead after all?

She was too afraid to hope, but she did anyway.

"No," he mumbled as if he knew exactly what she was thinking, and he stepped several inches away from her. "Before Gage died, he asked me to keep an eye on you. He made me promise."

His voice was like gravel, husky and raw, and Lynette studied what she could see of him. Tall. Lanky. He wore dark jeans, a black shirt and a black leather jacket.

There was a cowboy hat, also black, slung low on his forehead so that it was hard to see his face. He'd probably done that on purpose, since he was obviously trying to prevent her from getting a good look at him.

"Who are you?" she demanded.

He stepped deeper into the shadows. "It's best if you don't know my name."

"I disagree with that," Lynette snapped. "You're in my bedroom at four in the morning. How did you get in? All the doors and windows were locked, and I have a security system."

"I disarmed the system," he readily admitted. "And I'm pretty good at dealing with locks. Especially your locks. They're really kind of wussy, and you should look into upgrading."

He sounded cocky about that, and it made her trust him even less than she already did. Lynette wanted to scream again. Or at least get her gun so she could try to defend herself from this name-dropping intruder. Heck, he might not even know Gage. Maybe he'd just learned enough about her to realize that he could use Gage's name to get her to listen.

She didn't intend to listen for long.

"Go ahead," the man offered. He tipped his head to the drawer. "If holding a weapon on me will make you feel better, then do it."

Well, he was chock-full of surprises, but if this was some kind of reverse psychology, she wasn't biting. Lynette jerked open the drawer and grabbed the .38 as fast as she could. She didn't aim it at him, exactly, but she pointed it in his general direction. And she would take aim if he didn't give her some answers and give them fast.

"Start talking," she demanded.

He lifted his shoulder. "Gage said you'd probably want proof that he sent me," he casually tossed out there.

"I do." And then she would also want to know who this man was and why he was here.

The timing was certainly suspicious.

Dangerous, even.

"Gage told me a lot about you." That's all he drawled for several moments, and it was a drawl. Easy and cocky like the rest of him. "He said you owned the town newspaper, that you bought it a couple of years ago."

"So?" She tried to sound cocky, too, but failed. Her voice was shaking almost as much as her hand. Clearly, she wasn't as accustomed to break-ins as this guy was. "That's public record. Tell me something that isn't."

Another shoulder lift. "When Gage was twenty-one, he got Hodgkin's. Something very few people know."

True. At Gage's insistence that information had been limited to his family and the doctors in San Antonio who'd treated him. Still, that info alone wouldn't convince her to trust this man.

"Gage and you eloped when he was twenty-two and you were nineteen," he continued nearly right away. "But you had the marriage annulled a few weeks later because your father disapproved of the relationship."

Lynette's eyes narrowed. "You could have learned that from just about anyone who lives in Silver Creek. People here still gossip about it."

"Your father is Ford Herrington, a businessman and now a state senator, and he hated Gage," the man stated as if he hadn't heard her. "Your father thought you could do a lot better than a Ryland cowboy cop, and you caved in under the pressure and did as he wanted."

Now, she aimed the gun at him because these weren't very reassuring answers to prove that Gage had indeed sent him. "Again, not convincing. Any town gossip could have told you that."

But this intruder had managed to hit a nerve that was still raw after all these years. Because what he said was true.

Lynette had caved in.

"If this is all the proof you have, you can get out because this conversation is over," she informed him.

"It's not all I have."

He let that hang in the air for a few seconds before he stepped from the shadows, and she saw his face when he angled his head. He wasn't as young as she'd originally thought. There were some wrinkles around his eyes and on his forehead, and his neatly trimmed beard was flecked with gray.

"I need to get something from my pocket," he said, "and I'd rather you not shoot when I do that, okay?"

He waited until Lynette gave a crisp nod before he reached inside his leather jacket and took out the *something*. Whatever it was, it was small, but it made a plinking sound when he dropped it on the nightstand. Even though the room itself was dark, the outside security lights flickered off the white-gold circle.

It was Gage's wedding band.

Or one exactly like it.

Lynette picked it up with her left hand, keeping her gun in place in her right, and she reached out again to turn on the lamp.

"No." The man snagged her wrist. "Not a good idea."

That sent a chill through her, and she was about to ask why, but he released the grip he had on her, took a penlight from his pocket and handed it to her. It was small, as well, but it did the job. Lynette could see the etched swirls on the outside of the wedding band and the inscription inside: Gage's and her initials. And there was something else.

TLF.

"'True love forever,'" the man provided. He made a show of clearing his throat. "Cute. But not very accurate, huh? Two weeks isn't anywhere close to *forever*."

Lynette shot him a glare. Then, she swallowed hard. This man could have found the ring wherever Gage had last left it, looked into her past and then guessed what the initials meant. He could have done that for a variety of reasons—especially money. Maybe he thought he could get her to cough up cash for this part of her past.

But whatever was going on here, the ring itself was real. That was the ring she'd bought for Gage the day they got married.

"How did you get this?" she asked.

The man shrugged again. "Gage gave it to me. In case you needed to be convinced about him asking me to keep an eye on you."

"I still need convincing," Lynette assured him. "You knew Gage well?"

He nodded.

Lynette waited, then huffed. "I'd like a few details so I can tell if you're lying. How did you know him?" She had to take a breath to finish. "How did Gage die?"

"I worked with him in the CIA." He paused as if weighing each word carefully. "And you know how he died. The agency told you."

"No. The agency told his family. His five brothers. I got a phone call two days after the fact from his brother Grayson, who's the sheriff. All he said was that Gage had been killed while on a classified assignment at an undisclosed location. He didn't know anything else. Or maybe he just hadn't wanted to share it with me."

Even now, eleven months later, that was another slice to her heart. Of course, Lynette couldn't blame Grayson, since she hadn't exactly stayed on a friendly basis with the Rylands, and she couldn't very well tell them that the estrangement was for their own benefit.

And for their safety.

That would have only created questions that she couldn't answer. Still couldn't.

"Gage's last assignment was in South America," the man went on. "Things didn't go as planned, and we were ambushed. He was shot, and right before he died he gave me that ring and made me swear to keep an eye on you."

Oh, God.

Now, those were the details that felt real. And convincing. Painful, too. It felt as if someone had clamped a fist around her heart and was squeezing the life out of her. She couldn't breathe. And everything inside her started to spin.

"Gage is really dead?" All she could manage was a broken whisper to ask that question.

The man made a sound, something akin to a *duh*. "You knew that."

"Yes." But until this moment, Lynette had hoped and prayed that it wasn't true. She blinked back tears. "I know it now."

She fought the pain and the panic rising inside her. Later, she would grieve and try to come to terms with losing him. *Really* losing him. But first, she had to deal with her intruder. Despite the horrible news that he'd just delivered, she doubted he'd come here in person to confirm Gage's death. He could have done that with a phone call.

"Why would Gage ask you to keep an eye on me?" Lynette asked.

"Who knows? He was dying, and men don't always use their last breath to make a wise request."

She didn't miss the venom in his voice. Probably because he believed she'd done Gage wrong. And she had. But Lynette had had her reasons way back then, and she didn't intend to explain them to this man. Or anyone else.

Some secrets were best left secret.

"I did as Gage asked," the man continued as his glare drilled into her. "I kept an eye on you. I ran some cyber-searches. I even followed you a few times."

A chill rifled through her. Mercy. She hadn't noticed anyone following her in the eleven months since Gage's death. That shook her to the core. Because if this man could do that without her knowing, then others could have done it, as well.

"How much do you know?" she risked asking.

He stepped closer. "Enough to realize you're in way over your head." He paused. "Your father's a dangerous man, and he has dangerous allies. You've been digging into their files and business records, and I can promise you, that's not a good idea."

Lynette forced herself to remain calm. Well, on the outside anyway. Inside, there was a firestorm. There weren't many people who would have labeled her father as dangerous.

Powerful, yes.

Ruthless, even.

But Lynette and apparently this intruder were part of the small handful of people who suspected that her father was much, much more than the political facade that he'd created.

"I did look into his business dealings," she admitted. "But I stopped."

He stared at her, studying her. "Why?" His roughly barked question hung in the air.

"I decided other things were more important," she settled for saying.

"What things?" he snapped.

Confused at his intense emotion over what was a personal matter to her, Lynette shook her head. She had no intentions of telling him. "*Things* that have nothing to do with my father or with you."

"Tell me why you stopped." He paused between each word and spoke with clenched teeth.

Okay. That helped cut through the fear and the pain. A year ago she probably would have nicely tried to talk her way out of this, but there was a proverbial line drawn in the sand, and this cowboy had just crossed it.

Lynette got to her feet. "Enough is enough. So what if Gage asked you to keep an eye on me? Well, I don't want your eye or anything else on me. Get out now!"

She pointed the gun right at his chest.

He huffed and propped his hands on his hips. "What if I'm wearing a Kevlar vest, huh?"

Lynette blinked. "What?" And she wanted to ask if he'd missed a dose of meds or something. Because he was either ice-cold under pressure or he was crazy.

Another huff, and he grabbed the barrel of her gun and aimed it higher. "If I'm wearing Kevlar, then a chest shot will just temporarily knock the breath out of me, crack a rib or two and then piss me off. If I'm the big bad threat that you think I am, then go for a head shot. No Kevlar there."

Lynette just stared at him. "Who the heck are you?"

He leaned in so close that she caught the scent of the rain on his clothes.

And maybe something else…

"I'm the man who's going to save your life, darlin'," he growled. "And you'll let me do it because of that promise I made to Gage. You're going to take a suitcase from your closet, pack a change of clothes, and you'll leave with me *now*. We're moving fast, light and without any more arguments or questions from you."

He started to step back. Back into the shadows, but Lynette caught on to his arm and yanked him closer. Well, she tried anyway. He looked lanky, but the muscles in his arm were rock-hard and, despite the rough pull she'd given him, he didn't budge even a little.

Lynette reached to turn on the lamp again. She wanted a better look at his eyes to see if she could recognize something. *Anything*. But he ripped the lamp's electrical plug from the wall socket.

"I thought I made it clear—no light," he insisted. He pointed to the rain-streaked windows. "Because there could be someone bad out there. If he's not already here, he will be soon. And trust me, Gage didn't send this guy to keep an eye on you."

Lynette's gaze darted to the window, and she would have moved closer if the man hadn't latched on to her shoulder and anchored her in place.

"Who is this *someone* out there?" she demanded.

He cursed, and his grip melted off her. "A hired gun. And he has orders to kill you."

Chapter Two

Well, so far this plan just plain sucked.

Despite the near darkness, Gage Ryland could see the color drain from Lynette's face, and with her chest pumping for air, she sank back on the edge of the bed. Even with the bad blood and old baggage between them, he hated to see her like this. Frightened.

And in the worst kind of danger.

Maybe she would be frightened enough to cooperate, because Gage really had to get her out of there fast.

"You're lying," she said.

Denial. That was a predictable reaction. Too bad he didn't have time for it. "I wish," he mumbled.

While he was wishing, Gage wished he had a better plan, because this one *sucked*. It was taking too long, and there was way too much touching and close contact going on.

Too much emotion.

And Lynette wasn't the only one of them responsible for that. He hadn't expected this to feel like a bandage being ripped from a raw, unstitched wound. But that's exactly how it felt. This trip down memory lane wasn't doing his heart or his gut any good.

He should have just waited outside her house in the storm and killed the would-be killer, quietly disposed of the body and then kept watch for the next assassin that would come her way.

And there would be others.

He was sure of that.

It was the *there would be others* logic that Gage had used to justify putting on this middle-age disguise and risking everything to warn Lynette of the danger. Not just of this danger but of those assassins that would come even after he managed to neutralize this one.

Well, he'd warned her all right, along with feeding her a boatload of lies about a promise he'd made to a dead man.

No promise.

And the dead man was standing smack-dab in front of her.

Of course, Lynette couldn't learn either of those things tonight. Or ever. In the only way that mattered, Gage was dead to her, and it had to stay that way even if a little part of him wanted to confront her about the way she'd sliced and diced his heart all those years ago. But while a confrontation might make him feel marginally better, it wouldn't do much to help the situation.

Her closet door behind him was already open. Gage knew that because he'd opened it not long after he'd broken into her house, and he pulled out her overnight bag that he'd located on the shelf. But Lynette only pushed it away when he tried to hand it to her.

"Who's the hired gun and who sent him?" she demanded.

All right. The denial was already over. Well, maybe. At least she was asking questions again, and the sooner Gage furnished her with answers, the sooner he could convince her to leave this place and go into hiding. Best not to spend much time in this room with her.

Especially with her wearing a paper-thin white gown that hugged her body. A body he remembered a little too well.

Yeah.

He had to hightail it out of there ASAP.

"The hit man's name is Freddie Denton," Gage explained.

Thanks to a throat spray that the CIA used to help with disguises and covers, his voice was like a Texas gravel road. He didn't sound anything like himself.

He hoped.

Gage also hoped he could finish this rescue plan before the effects of the spray wore off. He figured he only had about an hour, tops, and the minutes of that hour were ticking away fast. Not good, since she was staring at him as if he'd lost his mind. She sure wasn't moving or doing what he'd told her to do.

He huffed and doled out some more details. "An informant called to let me know that Denton was on the move and making arrangements to pay you a visit."

"A visit?" she questioned.

Gage gave her a flat look that probably didn't translate well beneath the layers of prosthetic makeup and dark brown contacts. "Denton doesn't make social calls. He kills people for a living, and he's very good at what he does."

She kept her chin high, but her breathing was still way too fast. "Then if he's a known killer, why haven't you arrested him? Especially since you're a CIA agent, like Gage was."

Oh, man.

Yeah, it'd been years since he'd seen Lynette, but he didn't remember her being this, well, courageous or mouthy. He'd counted on her screaming—which she'd done—and then begging him to get her out of there. She hadn't exactly begged for the latter, but Gage would still do it.

However, these questions were eating into their escape time.

"No one has arrested Denton because he doesn't leave evidence behind, that's why," Gage settled for saying. "He kills witnesses and anyone else who gets in his way."

But Lynette only shook her head and kept staring at him.

Gage didn't bother with another huff. It was making his throat sore so he got started on something he'd wanted her to do. He put her overnight bag on the bed next to her.

"Pack," he insisted.

She didn't stop staring. "Convince me why I should."

This stubborn streak was getting old fast.

He got right in her face and slowed his words so that she would grasp each life-threatening one. "About two and a half hours ago Denton left his house in Houston, and he was armed with an assault rifle, night-vision goggles and a map to your house. It's my guess that with the rain-slick roads, he'll be here in five minutes."

Actually, it would probably be about fifteen, but Gage wanted to up the urgency here.

Her breath rattled in her throat. Because of the darkness, he couldn't clearly see her eyes, but Gage knew they were a deep ocean blue. And right about now, she would no doubt be fighting back tears and the terror. Lynette wasn't accustomed to hit men and danger. Prior to this, her father had kept her just out of reach of that.

Gage had tried to do the same.

But he'd failed.

This would be brutal, but she needed to hear it. "I figure Denton will do one of two things. He'll try to gun you down through that bedroom window the moment he arrives, or he'll just wait until morning when you walk out your front door to go to your car. Either way, you'll be dead…unless you leave with me right now."

Her forehead bunched up. "And who hired Denton?"

"I'm not sure—yet." Gage checked his watch. The minutes were ticking off fast. If he didn't convince her soon, he'd have to use the tranquilizer packet he had in his coat pocket. "I suspect it was your father or one of his slimeball business associates you were investigating."

Gage knew their names: Nicole Manning and Patrick Harkin. Names that Lynette already knew, as well, because *(a)* she'd known the pair most of her life, and *(b)* she'd been conducting a pseudo-investigation into some of their business deals that dated back as far as two decades.

Good intentions.

Bad idea.

Real bad.

"When you started playing Nancy Drew and digging into your father's records, I think it made Patrick and Nicole very nervous," Gage clarified. Since she wasn't packing yet, he did it for her. He grabbed the first outfit he could reach in her closet, jeans and a top, and stuffed them into the overnight bag. "One of them could have hired Denton. Or maybe your father decided to cut his losses and put a permanent end to your snooping."

"Not my father," she whispered. Lynette pulled in a long breath and repeated the denial. "He wouldn't send someone to kill me."

Gage could have argued that, but he'd learned the hard way he would just be wasting his breath. Lynette was never going to believe her father was the bottom-feeding monster that he truly was.

"Besides," she added. "I've already stopped looking into their records."

He studied her face to see if that was a lie. It wasn't. "When did you stop?"

She hesitated. "Nearly a month ago."

Gage didn't miss that little hesitation, but he let it pass for now. "Well, I don't think your daddy got the memo about that." He didn't bother to tone down the sarcasm. "And even if he did, he might have thought you were still too much of a liability."

He went to her dresser drawer, grabbed a handful of underwear. Yep, a lacy bra and panties similar to the ones that'd been tossed onto the chair in the corner, and he crammed the items into the bag.

"What exactly were you looking for in those records?" Gage asked her.

Her gaze snapped to him again, and she scowled. "It doesn't matter now. I'm no threat to my father or to Patrick or Nicole. I can call them and let them all know that."

Gage had to risk touching her again when Lynette reached for the phone. "And what will you say to them?" He got his hand off her as quickly as he could. *"Daddy, I know you hired a hit man to kill me, but I promise I'll be a good girl. Again,"* he added in a mumble.

Hell.

That was a fit-of-temper kind of response, and Lynette obviously latched right onto it. She stood, slowly, and stared at him. She also aimed her gun.

At his head.

She was a fast learner.

"I'm doing something I should have done the moment I found you in my bedroom," Lynette warned him. "I'm calling the sheriff."

Great. Just what he didn't need. His big brother Grayson in on this stupid-butted plan. That couldn't happen for a lot of reasons, so Gage grabbed her hand again when Lynette reached for the phone on the nightstand.

"You can't," he let her know.

"I can," she let him know right back. "If there's really a hit man on his way here, then the sheriff can stop him."

"Yeah. Or the sheriff can get killed by a pro who knows how to do just that." Grayson and he had never seen eye to eye, but Gage wasn't going to let Denton gun down his brother. Or for that matter gun down Lynette, despite this sudden stubborn streak.

Lynette tried to throw off his grip, and Gage had no choice but to grab on to her and put her against the wall.

The clicking sound surprised him.

It surprised the heck out of her, too.

Lynette's eyes widened, and she looked down at the trigger she'd just pulled. The gun was no longer aimed at his head. But rather the ceiling.

"Your bullets are in my pocket," he explained once he got his mouth working again. Sheesh. His heart was beating a mile a minute, and that didn't happen very often.

She made a sound of outrage and kept struggling to get away from him. "You unloaded my gun?"

"Yeah, before you woke up. And in hindsight, it was a smart move, don't you think?" Gage grabbed both her wrists in his left hand and shook the .38 loose in case she tried to bash him in the head with it.

"Hell," he grumbled. "I didn't think you'd actually pull the trigger."

And for some stupid reason, that nearly made him smile even though the aim at the ceiling meant she was just trying to fire a warning shot. Still, she'd fired. His ex had grown a spine. *Finally.* Under different circumstances and if her delays weren't a threat to their lives, he might have approved.

Gage's near smile went south though when she tried to knee him in the groin. She got darn close, too. Her kneecap rammed into his thigh and had him seeing stars.

"Time for the tranquilizer," he grumbled. He took out the plastic packet from his pocket.

"No!" Just like that, Lynette stopped struggling. "Please. No drugs. I'll do whatever you say."

Gage stopped, too, and he stared at her, trying to figure out what this was all about. "It's just a mild sedative. It won't hurt you. You'd be out ten minutes, tops."

"I don't want to be unconscious. It's a phobia I have." Lynette held his stare and put some steel in her voice. "Now, let go of me so we can leave. Denton will be here soon."

Yeah. And Gage was more than a little suspicious that Lynette had suddenly realized the need for them to get the heck out of there—especially since he hadn't made much headway with her until now with the tranquilizer threat.

Gage let go of her, stepped back, and with some major suspicion, he watched her grab the bra and panties from the chair and then go to the closet. He didn't think she had another gun in there, but she might try to use something to club him. Gage didn't believe for one minute that he'd actually convinced her that leaving was the only way for her to stay alive.

So, what was she up to?

Had she managed to find a weapon in that closet?

"Don't look," she insisted. "I want to put on some clothes."

Gage didn't look. Not exactly. But he didn't trust her enough to give her complete privacy.

Lynette somehow managed to get on the underwear

while her gown was still draped over her body. The gown finally hit the floor, and she immediately slipped into a loose blue dress. If there'd been time, he would have suggested jeans or something that covered more of her. But that would have required him seeing her half-naked again.

He was pretty sure that wasn't a good idea.

"I left my raincoat at my office, but I can use this," she explained, pulling a cherry-red trenchcoat from a hanger. She put it on over the dress and slipped on a pair of shoes.

Gage checked both, including the coat pockets. Too bad that required more touching. Those pockets were deep, and the search for a possible weapon sent his hand skimming against her thigh.

Oh, yeah. This plan sucked.

She huffed, maybe at the hand-to-thigh contact and mumbled something about him being a pervert. Lynette grabbed the overnight bag from the bed.

And Gage's wedding ring from the nightstand.

Something he'd been about to take for himself.

"If Denton comes in the house looking for me," Lynette mumbled, slipping the ring onto her index finger, "I don't want him to find it."

Neither did Gage, but he had to wonder why that was so important to Lynette. It couldn't be because she still had feelings for him.

No.

Couldn't be that.

She'd had their marriage annulled ten years ago, and the few times he'd seen her since, Lynette hadn't been just distant, she'd been downright ice-cold. Not just to him but to his family, as well. So, what was with her grabbing that ring?

Too bad Gage didn't have time to find out.

"What?" she asked, probably because he was staring holes in her. She moved closer.

Her gaze connected with his.

That kind of deep eye contact was something else that shouldn't happen. The *windows of the soul* theory might be all bunk, but he didn't want to risk Lynette seeing the real person behind those colored contacts and disguise.

"Let's go," Gage ordered. He picked up her gun and his penlight, stuffed them into his jacket pocket and led her out of the room and into the hall.

In his research he'd learned that Lynette had only owned the place two years, so this was Gage's first trip here. That's why he'd taken a couple of minutes to familiarize himself with the layout.

And even a few seconds to watch her sleep.

He wasn't proud of that. It had seemed more like a violation of her privacy than breaking in. After all, the breaking in had been necessary, but there was no logical explanation for why he'd nearly lost his breath when he'd seen her lying there in bed.

So many memories.

So many vivid images of her naked body.

She'd been right to call him a pervert.

Gage mumbled some profanity. Oh, good. Now, he was feeling hot in all the wrong places. Sadly, Lynette could do that to him even though his brain didn't want another dose of what she doled out. He'd barely survived their last showdown.

"How do we know Denton isn't already out there waiting for us?" Lynette asked.

It took Gage a moment to switch gears, which should have been a big fat clue for him to get his mind off her and back on the plan. "Because I left a sensor wire on the road

about an eighth of a mile from your house. If he'd driven
over it, the monitor in my jacket would have gone off."

"Assuming Denton stays on the road," she pointed out.

It was an assumption all right, but Gage was banking on the fact that Denton didn't know anyone was onto
him. Gage was also banking on the fact that he was just
as good of a shot as Denton. Maybe better. Still, he didn't
want to test that theory because it would mean Lynette
would be in the middle of a gunfight. The plan was for
her to stay alive, not to be shot in cross fire.

Gage pulled his weapon and expected the gasp he
heard Lynette make. "You said Denton wasn't here yet."

"It's just a precaution to have the gun ready," he explained.

But it might become a necessity. He wasn't walking
out that door without something to defend them.

They went through the dining room. Then the kitchen.
Gage kept his eye on Lynette in case she tried to grab a
knife or cast-iron skillet to club him over the head, and he
cracked open the back door. The rain and storm muffled
sounds he would have preferred to hear, but he didn't see
anything suspicious.

"Let's go," he ordered.

"On foot?" she asked. When she dug in her heels, Gage
took her by the arm and led her onto the porch.

"I left my vehicle on the Old Creek Road. About a five-
minute walk." Something she no doubt already knew.
"Eight minutes if you keep dragging your feet."

"I'm dragging my feet because I'm not sure I should
trust you."

"Yeah. I got that. You tried to shoot me, remember?"

"I tried to shoot the ceiling," Lynette snapped. "Not
you. But maybe I should have. After all, you broke in to
my house." She mumbled something he didn't catch. "Of

course, you made sure I couldn't shoot you. Just how long were you in my house before I woke up?"

Gage would take that secret to the grave, and if they didn't hurry, he might be in the grave, a real one, sooner than he'd imagined.

He tuned out her mumblings and protests and kept watch around them. When he was as sure as he could be that it was safe, Gage pulled her off the porch and onto the soggy ground.

The rain immediately assaulted them, and he hoped his disguise would last a little while longer. All he had to do was get her to his SUV and drive about ten miles to the small regional airport where he had a plane and pilot waiting to whisk her away to safety.

But *all he had to do* could be complicated in too many ways. Especially since she was still dragging her feet. Gage gave her a rough jerk to get her moving at more than a snail's pace.

"Gage wouldn't have asked a man like you to keep an eye on me," she snarled when he pulled her again.

He was about to assure Lynette that she was wrong, but the monitor inside his coat beeped.

Just one soft little sound.

But it was more than enough for him to know this plan was about to get a lot more dangerous. That's because Denton was ahead of schedule. He'd either driven like the wind or tagged someone else closer to come after Lynette, because Gage didn't think this was someone else paying a social call at this hour of the morning.

"Stay low and behind the trees," Gage warned her. Which shouldn't be hard since her backyard was littered with pecans and oaks.

He looked over his shoulder to make sure Lynette understood. But the only thing he saw was the wild fear in her eyes. Before he could even try to calm her down, she shocked the heck out of him.

She threw the overnight bag right at him.

Because Gage hadn't been expecting it, he rammed into a tree when the bag rammed into him.

And Lynette took off running.

Gage didn't take the time to curse or remind himself that he should have kept a closer watch on her. He just went after her, the mud and the rain sloshing all around his boots and probably doing a real number on his disguise.

Lynette was a lot faster than he'd figured she would be, maybe because she knew which mud holes and tree roots to dodge. Gage didn't. And he stumbled over a few before he finally managed to snag her by the shoulder. In the same motion, he dragged her behind the nearest tree.

"Let me go!" she said in an angry whisper. She punched at him again and tried to get away.

Oh, man. He didn't have time for this. Gage kept her tight in his grip and reached in his pocket for the tranquilizer. He couldn't risk Denton hearing her and coming straight into the backyard. It would prevent them from escaping, and he didn't want to hide out for what could be a half hour or more in the rain and behind a tree with a woman hell-bent on beating the tar out of him.

"This will keep you calm," he promised her, ripping open the packet of the liquid sedative. And it'd make her temporarily unconscious—a real bonus right now. "It'll be safer carrying you than chasing you down."

"No. Please." Lynette frantically shook her head and shoved away the packet that contained the drug-soaked cloth. "You can't. It might hurt the baby."

Now, it was Gage who froze.

"Baby?" he spit out. "What baby?"

Chapter Three

Lynette hadn't intended to blurt out her baby news.

She hadn't wanted a soul to know that she was pregnant. Not yet anyway. But she couldn't allow this man to use a tranquilizer or any other drug on her. At this early stage of her pregnancy, she had no idea what kind of damage it could do to her unborn child. It might even cause her to miscarry.

The man glared at her, and Lynette didn't know why her baby news would cause him to react this way. Nor did she care. She was tired of fighting. Tired of this man. And tired of the entire situation of hit men and danger. If he was so determined to get her to safety, then Lynette was going to cooperate.

Well, maybe.

If she got a chance to escape again, she would take it in a heartbeat, but she wouldn't do that if it meant further risk to her child.

"Denton?" she reminded him when he just stood there gawking at her. "He tripped the sensor, remember? And that means he'll be here any minute."

He shook his head as if to clear it and caught on to her arm again. "Yeah."

Yeah? That was his only explanation for his extreme reaction about her pregnancy? It certainly didn't mesh

with the smart-mouthed cockiness that he'd shown her up
to this point. Unless he was planning on doing something
or taking her somewhere that wouldn't be safe for a pregnant woman. Of course, a hit man wouldn't be safe, either.

"Come on," he finally snarled.

The return of the surly tone was actually a relief. Sort
of. But it was more of a relief when he caught on to her
arm again. For a moment Lynette thought they might start
running. After all, a hit man on their tails warranted running. But he kept the pace at a light jog as they slogged
their way through the mud and grass.

Maybe he was being considerate now that he knew
she was pregnant. Or maybe things weren't as urgent as
she'd thought.

The slash of light changed her mind about the *lack of
urgency* and robbed Lynette of what little breath she'd
managed to keep.

Headlights.

No doubt belonging to Denton's vehicle.

Well, they were Denton's headlights all right *if* this
mouthy intruder had told her the truth. Lynette couldn't
be sure about him. Something definitely wasn't right, but
she didn't know what. Still, if he'd wanted her dead, he
could have managed that before she ever woke up.

Not exactly a comforting thought.

The headlights of the approaching vehicle suddenly
went dark, causing her heart to pound even harder. Her
intruder had no reaction. Not even slightly tensed muscles. And she could tell that because he practically had
her in a bear hug as they jogged.

"Denton's out of his car," the man mumbled.

Lynette had no idea how he knew that, especially since
they were a good twenty yards from the house and even
farther from the road. Added to that, it was still pitch-

dark. But then, there was another light. A tiny streak that had the man mumbling some profanity.

"He has a flashlight," he whispered. And he yanked her behind the nearest tree.

He positioned her so that the front of her body was against the towering pecan. He pressed himself against her back, and he was big enough that he created a shield of sorts.

They waited there, the seconds crawling by, with her heartbeat crashing in her ears and the rain swiping at them with each gust of wind. The man, her self-proclaimed protector, kept his gun ready and aimed, the barrel sticking out just slightly from the tree trunk.

"It's Denton all right," he whispered.

Lynette tried to blink the rain from her eyes so she could pick through the darkness and see what had made the muscles in her *protector*'s chest and arm turn to iron. Now that the headlights were off, she could no longer spot the car.

But thanks to her security lights that rimmed the eaves of her house, she saw the shadowy figure.

A man dressed in dark clothes. And he was indeed carrying a rifle.

Her stomach clamped into a hard knot. Lynette had held out hope that Denton wasn't real, or that he wasn't an actual hit man, but that rifle proved otherwise.

Sweet heaven.

What was she going to do?

She hadn't had time to finish her backup plan to move from Silver Creek, and now it might be too late. Denton could complicate things because once this was over, there'd be an investigation. She'd have to call the authorities. And that would mean bringing in Gage's family. There was no way she could keep the intruder's visit a secret.

"Keep quiet," the man warned her in a whisper. "And don't you dare think about running again." He kept his attention pinned to Denton.

Lynette had indeed considered running again, but she had to pick her poison here. An intruder or a likely hit man.

Some choice.

It was the intruder. *For now.*

She watched as Denton skulked toward the house. Straight toward her bedroom window. He lifted the rifle and fired, the bullets crashing through the glass panes.

Lynette clamped her hand over her mouth to muffle the gasp. The blasts slammed through her and robbed her of her breath and any hope that all of this had been some scare tactic. If she'd been inside, those bullets would have ripped through her. She'd be dead right now.

The man behind her made an *I told you so* sound. But that sound had no sooner left his mouth than he sucked in a quick breath. And Lynette knew why.

Denton looked inside the window, his face right against the now gaping hole that his bullets had left. He pulled back his shoulders, and then his gaze skirted all around the yard.

Oh, mercy.

He'd apparently realized that he'd just shot at her empty bed.

Lynette prayed that Denton would go inside, and then she and her Gage-appointed protector could get out of there. That rifle could fire just as deadly a shot into the yard as it had into the house.

"Get ready to move," the man whispered when Denton stepped onto her back porch.

Lynette did. Well, she got as ready as she could considering the ground was practically a mud bog and that her nerves were in shambles. The moment that Denton stepped inside her house, she and the man started to run. And this time, it wasn't a jog.

They *ran*.

The security lights didn't give them much illumination this far out, and it was next to impossible to see where they were running. Lynette hoped they didn't trip and fall.

The sound nearly caused her to do just that.

It was a thick blast, and it ripped through the darkness. Not from inside the house. No. It was much worse than that. This shot had been fired outside and in their direction.

The man latched on to her arm and pulled her behind another tree. Just in the nick of time. A shot slammed into the trunk of the oak and sent a spray of splinters everywhere.

Lynette couldn't think, couldn't breathe. She could only pray that the shots would miss and would end soon. Every bullet was a risk to her, her baby, and yes, even to this man she didn't completely trust.

Again, the man positioned himself so that he was shielding her, except this time he was pressed even harder against her until he had her flattened against the tree.

He reached out with his right hand and returned fire.

Since his gun was so close, just inches from her head, the blast was deafening. Lynette put her hands over her ears. Too late. Everything inside her was clanging, and that only revved up her fear and adrenaline.

Denton fired another shot into the tree.

Then another.

With each one Lynette knew this nightmare was real. But why? Why had someone sent Denton after her? Yes, she'd looked into those business deals in her father's files, but she hadn't found anything that incriminated Patrick, Nicole or even her father. She certainly hadn't found anything that would warrant her death.

Unless…

Oh, God. Was that it?

Did this have to do with her pregnancy? Had her father learned the secret that she'd paid dearly to have hidden? If so, then Denton was the least of her worries.

"Level your breathing," the man warned her. "Or you'll hyperventilate."

Lynette tried to do that. She tried to stop herself from spiraling into a panic, but it was hard to remain calm when this close to death. If she died, so did her precious baby.

"Stay ahead of me," he ordered.

Lynette had no idea what he meant by that until he shoved her away from the tree and in front of him. He pushed her to start running again. And that's exactly what Lynette did. She ran with him behind her, once again acting as her human shield. Gage must have somehow convinced this guy to risk taking a bullet for her.

But why?

Why had Gage thought of her safety during his last moments on earth?

Later, that was something she wanted to know. If this man would tell her, that is. So far, he'd been short on explanations and long on details that anyone could have learned. But Lynette had to know—had Gage somehow managed to forgive her during those last moments of his life?

Was this man the proof of that forgiveness?

If Gage had managed that, it wouldn't ease her immediate grief, but it might help with other things.

She slid her hand over her stomach.

Another shot.

Lynette braced herself for one of them to be hit, but this shot also slammed into the tree. Her rescuer had no doubt planned it that way because he kept them weaving in and out of the clump of trees, using them and his body to keep her out of the path of Denton's bullets.

"Watch out for the ditch," he reminded her.

Good thing, too, because Lynette had forgotten about it, though she'd walked near it dozens of times. Falling at this point could be a fatal mistake. They leaped over the foot-wide ditch and kept running.

Too bad the shots kept coming their way.

"Denton will have to reload soon," he let her know. "And then he'll run after us."

That didn't help keep her breathing level. Lynette didn't want to believe him, but unfortunately, he'd been right about everything so far. Maybe when this was done and they were safely out of here, he would tell her more *right* things. Like how she could stop this from happening again.

Just like that, the shots stopped. Apparently it was reloading time. And Lynette and the man automatically sped up, going from a jog to a sprint.

She was thankful that she was in good shape, and the irony was just the day before she'd asked her doctor if it was okay to continue jogging. He'd given her the green light. However, her obstetrician certainly wouldn't recommend her running for her life to dodge a hail of bullets.

The man shoved aside some low-hanging cedar branches and pulled her into the dense shrubs and underbrush at the edge of her property line. Though it was late September, everything was in full leaf, and the foliage scratched and slapped at her. Still, she felt safer here than out in the open.

Well, she felt safer until the shots started again.

And yes, Denton was indeed following them. These shots were closer than the others had been.

They broke through the wall of thick shrubs, and Lynette spotted the dark waters of the creek coiling around the rock and sand banks. She also spotted the dark-colored SUV. It was parked on the narrow dirt road—exactly where the man had said it would be. Another truth in his favor.

But they didn't head toward the SUV.

Much to her surprise, he latched on to her arm and practically dragged her into a clump of hackberries. Lynette was about to remind him that the idea was for them to get the heck out of there, but he put his mouth right against her ear.

"Denton's too close to us for us to escape," he whispered. He positioned them side by side so that he had a good angle to view the dirt road and the SUV. "If I start the engine, he'll hear it."

Lynette shook her head. "But you could drive out of here fast." In fact, she was going to insist on it. The farther and faster away from Denton, the better.

"The road's too straight for that. Denton could, and will, disable the SUV by shooting out the tires, and then we'd be forced to get out while he still has a rifle trained on us."

That sounded, well, logical. Something she didn't want to hear right now. Lynette didn't want logic. She wanted to get out there and away from the assassin trying to kill them.

"Just wait," he added in that same hoarse whisper. "If Denton comes this way, I'll see him." He paused so long that it drew Lynette's gaze up to his. "I'd prefer him alive so he can tell me the name of the scumbag who hired him."

Yes. Lynette hadn't considered that, but it was something she needed to know. That was the first step in stopping this and keeping her baby safe.

But would Denton tell them?

Maybe if this man pressed him, and Lynette didn't care how hard he pressed. She didn't care if he beat Denton to within an inch of his life. She had to know what had brought all of this down on her.

So, they sat and waited. With her breath racing. Her heart pounding. And the fear, overwhelming. She had to get out of this alive.

Because the hackberry trees were choked together, they actually created an umbrella of sorts, and they got a reprieve from the rain. His Stetson helped, too, because she was tucked partly beneath its brim. Still, despite the trees and her trenchcoat, she was soaked to the bone because she hadn't taken the time to button up. Maybe it was the chill and the adrenaline, but Lynette's teeth started to chatter.

"Shh," the man warned.

When the chattering only got worse, he hooked his left arm around her and pulled her inside his leather jacket and against his body.

Instant warmth. And comfort. Something she hadn't expected from this stranger.

Lynette drew her knees up to her chest and buried her face into the heat from his chest and shoulder. It didn't calm her exactly, but it helped. So did the fact that he had those diligent eyes trained on the area around them.

The rain made it hard to hear anything, but she listened for any sound that might alert them that Denton was near.

And she heard it.

The snap.

As if someone had stepped on a twig.

The man no doubt heard it, as well, because she felt the muscles in his arm tense just slightly. Barely a reaction and a drop in the bucket compared to hers. He eased away from her, probably to get ready to fire, and Lynette readied herself, as well. She pulled in her breath.

Taking in the man's scent.

Not the rain-slick leather jacket or even the T-shirt beneath.

She took in *his* scent.

Despite hearing that twig snap, Lynette looked up at the man. It was too dark to see his face, but she tried to recall every detail of it when she'd seen him in her bedroom. The wrinkles around his eyes, the gray in his beard and hair. None of those things was familiar.

But his scent was.

It stirred through her, warming her in a different kind of way than his body had. But then, Lynette shook her head.

No.

It couldn't be.

She stared at him, trying to see something in his face that would match the scent, but the sound had her attention snapping away from him. There was rustling movement in the underbrush to their right.

Just a split second of sound.

Before Denton came crashing through.

Denton pivoted, turning that rifle right on them. Her heart stopped. Her breath froze in her lungs. But the man with the familiar scent didn't freeze. He bracketed his right wrist with his left hand. Took aim.

And he fired.

He pulled the trigger twice, and even though Lynette

couldn't see exactly where the shots had gone, a few moments later, she had her answer. She saw Denton crumple into a heap on the ground.

"Hell," the man grumbled.

He kept his gun aimed at Denton, stood and cautiously went closer to the hit man. He bent down, touched his fingers to Denton's neck and added another *hell.* "He's dead."

Dead. Not exactly good news, because he wouldn't be able to tell them who'd hired him. As bad as that was, Lynette still didn't wish him alive.

But she did want something else.

She had to know.

Lynette stood and stepped from the cover of the hackberries. The rain immediately slapped at her, just as it was doing to the man in the black leather jacket and Stetson. She walked closer and drew in his scent again.

Oh, God.

She hadn't said that aloud, but he must have sensed some change in her body language.

"What?" he snapped, staring down at her.

Lynette shook her head and stared back. She was terrified to speak. But there was no chance she could stay silent and not ask the question.

"Gage?"

Chapter Four

Oh, hell.

This rescue had just gotten a lot more complicated.

Gage shook his head and tried to cut off the complication at its proverbial knees. But Lynette only shook her head, too, and she reached up and touched his face. Or rather she touched the thin sheet of prosthetic makeup that had created the wrinkles around his eyes and the fake beard.

"Gage," she repeated on a rise of breath.

And it definitely wasn't a question.

Since she looked ready to rip the rest of the makeup off his face, Gage took Lynette's arm and practically dragged her to the SUV. He had a lot to do now, more than he'd originally planned, and he doubted he could dodge her question for long. Especially since she seemed so darn sure of who he was.

But how the devil had she known?

This disguise had fooled enemy agents. Heck, it could have probably fooled his brothers. So, how did Lynette figure it out while running for her life from a hit man?

"Gage," she repeated when he stuffed her into the passenger's seat.

Gage groaned and hurried, getting behind the steering wheel as fast as he could. He had to put some distance between them and the hit man in case the guy had brought backup with him.

"You're alive." Lynette's breath broke, and a hoarse sob tore from her throat. She clawed at the prosthetics, ripping them off.

"Hold that thought," Gage told her. He wasn't completely immune to the emotion, or the fallout that would happen from this, but he had to make a call. Then, he'd figure out a way to deal with Lynette.

It wasn't going to be pretty.

He pressed the button on the secure phone on the dash, and his handler, Sherman Hendricks, answered on the first ring.

"Lock on to my coordinates," Gage instructed. "I just left a dead body in the woods, and I need the area to be sanitized. There's also an overnight bag near the residence, and it'll have to be moved."

In other words, a full cleanup of the dead assassin and the overnight bag in case his prints were on it. No one could know Gage had been there.

Well, no one except Lynette.

Gage didn't see a way around this big discussion that Lynette and he were about to have, so he ended the call to start some damage control.

"How did you know?" Gage was unable to stop himself from asking. He was good at his job. Damn good. And it was a little insulting that a civilian had figured it out in under a half hour.

"Your scent," she said in a breathy whisper.

Gage gave his armpit a quick smell but clearly didn't detect what Lynette had.

"No one else has that scent," she clarified, which of course, didn't clarify it much. She bolted across the seat and threw her arms around him. "It's you. It's really you."

Well, that wasn't the reaction Gage had expected.

Nor was the hungry kiss she planted on his mouth.

Her lips tasted of the rain and the salt from her tears. And of Lynette. Yeah, after all this time, he remembered exactly how she tasted. So, maybe it wasn't too much of a stretch for her to remember his scent.

Considering though that they hated each other, it was still a puzzling memory to latch onto.

The kiss continued, punctuated with her sobs and mumbles, and Gage finally had no choice but to pull over. Not a good time for it, with the body of a hit man only a mile away, but he didn't want to wreck.

Without thinking it through, Gage kissed her right back, that taste coiling through him. Oh, man. He'd missed her almost as much as he hated her.

Almost.

However, he was having a hard time remembering the hatred part while playing lip-lock with his ex. He kissed her far harder and deeper than he should have, but then considering he shouldn't be kissing her at all, he was getting his money's worth from this particular mistake.

Thankfully, the kiss didn't last much longer. Just seconds. Before Lynette stopped and pushed away from him.

"You let me think you were dead!" she shouted. And she planted both her hands against his chest and gave him a hard shove. "How could you do something like that to me? How?"

It took Gage a moment to recover from the scalding kiss, the shove and the quick change in Lynette's mood. "I had no choice."

"No choice?" she howled. The tears streamed down her cheeks. And she gave him another shove. "Everyone has a choice, Gage, and you let me and your family believe you were dead."

She stopped cold, stared at him. "Or does your family know the truth?"

He shook his head. "They don't. There are only two people who know—you and the man I just called." And for some very dangerous reasons, it had to stay that way.

Lynette cursed. Shoved him again. "You jerk!" And then she called him something worse. *Much* worse. "How could you do that to us?"

"How? I did it to save all of your lives!" And he immediately hated the outburst. Hated that he felt bad for the lies that had been necessary. "You think it was easy for me to give up my life? My family?"

He didn't add Lynette's name to that little tirade, felt a little guilty about it, and then Gage reminded himself that she was pregnant with another man's child.

Hell.

He'd only been fake dead for eleven months. Of course, Lynette and he hadn't been anything close to a couple for years. Ten years to be exact. But Gage was still riled even if he didn't have a right to be.

For that matter, Lynette didn't have a right to be riled, either. He reminded himself of that, too, and put some steel back in his attitude. Except he didn't have time to put that attitude into a mind-your-own-business snarl because she spoke before he could.

"Why did you do this?" she demanded. Now, she was the one with attitude.

Gage debated mentioning that part about her not having riling rights for anything related to him, but he didn't want this to launch into a long argument. He had to give her a quick, sterile explanation, so he could get her to the airport for the trip to safety. Then, he'd be out of her life.

Again.

And he didn't want to know why that suddenly didn't

feel like the perfect solution that it had been just thirty minutes ago.

Oh, wait. He did know.

It was because of that blasted kiss.

Sheesh. When the heck would he learn to quit thinking with any other organ that wasn't his brain? Because the rest of his body, especially parts of him that were still affected by Lynette, wasn't prone to making good decisions.

"Well?" she pressed. "I deserve an answer."

No, she didn't deserve anything from him, but he'd give her one anyway.

Mostly, it would be the truth.

"When I was on assignment last year, I killed a notorious international drug dealer, Rodney Dalvetti."

While he thought about how to continue, how to word this, Gage put the SUV in gear and started driving. He also picked off the rest of his now worthless disguise.

"Since Rodney had murdered a hundred people or more," he explained, "I didn't take his death too hard. But his brother, Sampson, did. Turns out Sampson's plenty upset about losing his rabid sibling, and he blames me for the shoot-out that his brother started."

Lynette used the heels of her hands to swipe away the tears. "This Sampson Dalvetti is after you?"

"*Was.* And when he couldn't find me, he swore that he'd come after my family. You, too, since he had his minions dig around and find out that we'd once been married." He shot her a glance. "I guess he figured he'd use anyone and everyone to draw me out so he could kill me."

"Oh, God," Lynette mumbled.

"Yeah, that was pretty much my reaction, but I added a lot more words when I heard what was going down."

Gage could protect himself, but he had five brothers, four sisters-in-law and a handful of nieces and nephews.

Plus, Lynette. That was a lot of people to try to protect, and he knew that sooner or later, Sampson would get to one or more of them. Gage also figured that Lynette would be at the top or near the top of Sampson's kill list.

Well, maybe.

Sampson had made it clear with his threats that he would take out Lynette. Gage wasn't sure why Sampson had locked in on her, especially since Gage had had little communication with her since the annulment. But that was a question for another day. A day when he had Lynette tucked away so that Sampson couldn't reach her.

"The only way I could keep you all safe was for Sampson to believe I was dead," Gage spelled out for her.

Still staring at him, she stayed quiet a moment. "You could have told me the truth," she whispered. "I would have kept your secret."

He shook his head. "Couldn't risk it." Though he had considered it. Well, he'd considered telling his brother Grayson, so he could make sure Sampson stayed away from Silver Creek. But in the end Gage had decided he was best suited to do that. And he had. That's how he'd learned about Denton targeting Lynette.

Lynette swiped away more tears, and she looked so sad, so distraught, that it had Gage shaking his head.

"I figured it wouldn't matter to you if I was dead or not," Gage reminded her. "Especially since I've been out of your life a long time now."

And he glanced at her stomach in case she missed the snarky reference.

Her eyes widened, and she got that deer-in-the-headlights look before she dodged his gaze completely. "But yet you came back to save me from a hit man." Another pause. Another headshake. "Why?"

And she didn't sound appreciative. But cautious. Afraid, even.

What the heck was going on in her mind?

The immediate danger was behind them. He'd gotten her out of there, and he would take the final step to ensure her safety. So, why the feeling that there was something else going on here?

"Why save me?" she repeated.

Again, Gage chose his words carefully. "My handler, the person I just called," he clarified, "got word from an informant that Freddie Denton had been hired to take you out. I needed to make sure he wasn't connected to Sampson so I came."

"And was Denton connected?" she pressed.

Gage shook his head. "I don't think so."

Of course, that didn't explain why Gage had come himself to take on this particular assignment. His handler could have sent another agent. But Gage had wanted to do this. One last thing for Lynette. Not because he felt he owed her. No way. However, he'd thought this would finally close those old wounds.

So far, he was batting a big fat zero in that wound-closing department.

"You're sure Denton's not connected to Sampson Dalvetti?" Lynette asked.

He got his thoughts back on track and hoped they stayed there. "I can't be positive, but the money trail for Denton's payment doesn't have international origins. Dalvetti usually deals with banks in the Cayman Islands."

"He could have made an exception to throw you off his scent," she pointed out.

Gage lifted his shoulder. "Yeah. But I verified that Dalvetti still believes I'm dead. There'd be no reason to come after you unless he's pretending to believe that I faked my death."

Now, it was Gage's turn to pause. "Of course, that leaves your father and his business associates. One of them could have hired Denton."

She made a sound of agreement, nothing else, and Gage took the turn to the small country airport. Lynette obviously noticed the route, knew where it led, but she didn't say anything. Maybe that meant she wouldn't give him any lip about getting on the plane that was waiting for her.

"Denton knew where your bedroom was in the house," he tossed out there. "He didn't look around. He got out of his vehicle, walked straight to the window and fired." And he gave her some time to think about that. "Dalvetti's never been to your house."

She shook her head, sucked in her breath. "Maybe he broke in, studied the layout and told Denton?"

Gage copied her headshake. "If Dalvetti had broken in, he would have kidnapped you. As a minimum." More likely, he would have killed her on the spot. "I doubt Denton got your floor plan from Dalvetti, and I know Denton didn't arrive any earlier to case the place."

Lynette stayed quiet a moment. "So, someone told Denton where my bedroom is."

Oh, yeah. "Someone who knew the floor plan."

"Someone who knew *me*," she corrected. "Someone who's been to my house."

Bingo.

"I've narrowed it down," Gage continued when Lynette didn't say anything about the accusation he'd just tossed out there about her father. "Of course, your dad, Ford, is tops on the list of suspects who could have hired Denton. But I haven't been able to rule out Patrick or Nicole."

Another sound of agreement, but like before, that was the only thing Lynette volunteered. Of course, she already knew what these people were capable of. Both Patrick and Nicole were ruthless in business and their personal lives. Ford was a couple of steps past the ruthless part. Except Lynette might disagree with that. She'd certainly jumped to defend her father when he'd torn them apart.

"All three have been to your house?" he asked.

"Yes," she verified after a huff.

"None of them would approve of you snooping in their dirty dealings. So, why did you?" Gage came right out and asked. Maybe this time, he'd get a real answer and not more of those noncommittal sounds. The woman was nearly as good at dodging the truth as he was.

In addition to that sound, which put his teeth on edge, Lynette shivered, prompting Gage to turn up the heat. And he waited. Waited some more. Then, more. Until time was just ticking away.

He cleared his throat and repeated his question. "Why?"

Still, she took more long moments before she opened her mouth. Moments they didn't have. "After you died… after I *thought* you died," she corrected, "I decided it was time to try to figure out exactly what my father and his associates were doing."

The explanation stopped there. Cold and way incomplete. "Why didn't you just find a rattlesnake or two to play with? It would have been safer."

That earned him a glare. "Because I wanted to know the truth about my father."

Wow. Not something he'd expected her to say. "Can you deal with the truth?" he fired back.

Her glare got worse but then softened almost immediately. "I was looking for proof that he had something to do with my mother's death."

Yeah, Gage knew something about that. Her mother had died from a so-called accidental drowning when Lynette was just a kid, nine years old. A lot of people had wondered if Ford had killed his wife, Sandra, after rumors of an affair.

Rumors of an affair between Sandra and Gage's own grandfather, Chet McLaurin, who was then the sheriff of Silver Creek.

Even now, after all these years, it hurt to think about losing his Granddaddy Chet. The rumors hurt, too. Though his grandfather had been a widower during the alleged affair, it had put a stain on his good name when folks whispered about a possible involvement with a married woman. And not just any married woman but the wife of the rich and powerful Ford Herrington.

"Did you find anything about your mother?" Gage pressed.

"No." She looked at him. "And I didn't find any link to my father killing your grandfather, either."

That didn't mean it hadn't happened.

The timing was suspicious since his grandfather had been gunned down by an unknown assailant just weeks after her mother's drowning. It was bad enough that during that same month Lynette and he had both lost people close to them, but then shortly after, Gage's own father had abandoned the family. Boone Ryland had just walked out without warning. Gage and his brothers had been devastated. Their mother, too, since she committed suicide not long after he left.

A lot of bad things had gone on around that time.

And Gage figured Ford Herrington could have started

the whole ugly ball rolling by killing his wife and her supposed lover.

"That was the worst summer of my life," Lynette mumbled. "Well, one of the worst. Another was when you got Hodgkin's." And she sounded all torn up about it.

He had to be wrong about that. These old memories couldn't mean anything to her now. If they had, then she would have tried to contact him during the past decade. She hadn't. And after a couple of years of waiting for that, Gage had shut out all thoughts of her.

Until now.

Hard to shut her out when she was just inches away and after that kiss.

"Even though you were sick, there were still some parts about that summer that were good," she said, her voice practically soundless. But somehow Gage managed to hear her anyway.

"Oh, you considered the good part our marriage?" he growled. "Except it didn't last long enough for the ink to dry on the license. Not much good about that."

No glare from her this time. Something he figured that she'd toss at him. In fact, it was the opposite reaction. Her forehead bunched up, and she started to nibble on her bottom lip.

"You hate my father because he forced me to get that annulment," Lynette mumbled.

Gage couldn't argue with that. It was true. But it was also true that he hated Lynette for not standing up to the man. Ford got away with what he did only because Lynette had allowed him to have his way. She'd backed down when Gage had needed her to stand up to her father.

Gage decided to take this conversation in a slightly different direction—or rather a backtracked one. His SUV was quickly eating up the miles to the airport, and while the conversation made him feel marginally better, it wasn't giving him the answers that he might be able to use to get to the bottom of this.

"I take it you didn't find any dirt on your mucked-up dad?" he concluded. "But we both know there's plenty of dirt to find. How hard and how long did you look?" Better yet, what had she found?

"There is dirt. I'm sure of it. But I didn't find it in any of the files in his office." She paused. More lip nibbling. Another pause. "I even tried taping him in the hopes that he might let something slip, but he must have known something was up, because he grabbed my purse and found the recorder that I'd tried to hide."

Of course, he would have. Ford was very good at reading people, and he was suspicious by nature. At least that's how Gage remembered him and all the dirty looks and snide comments he'd made when Lynette and he were dating.

But Ford had another side, that fake face he put on for the world to see. Gage had also gotten a glimpse of that when they'd first told Ford about their elopement. Maybe because they'd told him in front of witnesses, including the justice of the peace, Ford had been all calm on the outside. But there must have been some fire beneath all that calmness or else he wouldn't have talked Lynette into the annulment.

"Why'd you quit looking for the dirt on your father?" Gage asked. "And don't get me wrong— I'm glad you quit. Less snooping will keep you alive. But why'd you try to close up Pandora's box after you opened it?"

"I had my reasons," she snapped.

And apparently those were reasons that she wasn't planning to share with him. He'd probably find out anyway, because he was going to do some deep digging of his own when he had Lynette on safe ground.

Gage pulled into the tiny airport parking area, stopped and spotted the plane on the runway. Good. No hitch in that department. The pilot was there, as well, tucked underneath the awning of the maintenance hangar. In other words, this last leg of the plan was a go—despite the rocky start with the hit man and the kiss. What Gage should do was get Lynette's butt on the plane *now* and never look back.

But the need for those answers gnawed away at him, and he just couldn't let go of it yet. Especially one answer in particular.

"And what would those reasons be for stopping the investigation?" he pressed, and he braced himself for another snapped response.

Which he didn't get.

With her mouth tight, she just stared out at the wipers slashing the rain off the windshield.

"Okay. You won't tell me," he fired back. "Then, let me guess. You fell in love with someone. Or maybe it wasn't love. Maybe just lust. You landed in the sack with him, and when you found out you were pregnant, you figured you'd better not do anything to get yourself and that baby killed."

More silence.

That didn't help the anger roaring inside him. "At least tell me that this SOB is willing to marry you now that you're pregnant."

"We haven't discussed it," she mumbled.

Gage cursed. "Was this like a one-night stand?" He didn't wait for an answer. Which he should have. He also should have dropped a subject that was none of his business. But he didn't. He just had to get in one more jab to go along with the knot that this news had put in his gut.

"There is such thing as safe sex, you know?"

Even though Gage wasn't too happy about any kind of sex with Lynette that didn't involve him. Yeah. That was petty since they weren't together. Heck, they didn't even like each other anymore.

Still, it stung.

This pregnancy was a couple of steps past stinging. Maybe because part of him—the immature part still hanging on to the past—remembered that once, years ago, Lynette and he had planned to have kids of their own.

A whole brood of them, she'd insisted. To make up for her being an only child.

Gage had siblings, five of them, so he didn't have the same need as Lynette did, but yeah, he'd wanted kids back then. Now… Well, *now* didn't matter. His future was sealed as long as Sampson Dalvetti was alive, and since Gage hadn't been able to get to him in the past eleven months, he wasn't counting on eliminating the drug lord anytime soon.

Lynette pointed to the plane. "I'm supposed to get on that?" she asked.

It took a moment to get his jaw unclenched, and it didn't happen until after he cursed himself for going off on another thought tangent. "You are. You're supposed to stay gone until I can figure out who's trying to kill you."

She pulled back her shoulders. "You mean you're continuing the investigation into my father and the others?"

"Damn straight." It was the only way to end this.

Lynette shook her head. "It's too dangerous. If my father learns you're alive—" Again, she stopped cold.

And Gage intended to find out why this was a forbidden subject with her. She knew how he felt about Ford.

Gage hated the man, and the feeling was mutual. There was no reason for her to keep skirting around the obvious.

"You think your father will try to kill me?" Gage concluded. "Well, that's a chance I'll have to take, because if I don't stop him, or the person responsible, then you'll never be safe. You'll never be able to have a normal life. Guys like Freddie Denton will just keep coming after you."

She frantically shook her head. "I won't be safe if my father finds out you're alive. He'll put things together. He'll start digging."

Lynette sucked in her breath as if she'd said too much.

But she hadn't said nearly enough.

Fed up with the lack of answers, Gage caught her by the shoulders and turned her toward him. "I know Ford hates my guts, but why would my being alive make your father come after *you?*"

She tried to dodge his gaze, tried to turn away from him, but Gage held on, and he got right in her face. "Why?" he demanded.

She started shaking her head and didn't stop. "I can't."

"Yes, you can." And Gage didn't say it nicely. "If you don't tell me, I'll get the answer from your father."

Lynette gasped. "Please. You can't," she repeated. "It'd only make things worse."

Probably, but it was just a bluff. Still, that didn't mean he was going to let her get on that plane until he had what he wanted. An answer.

"Why would your father come after you if he finds out I'm alive?" he pushed. Gage glared at her, to let her know he wasn't just going to let this go.

Her gaze came to his, finally, and it seemed as if Lynette changed her mind a dozen times before she opened her mouth. "Because my father will figure things out about the baby."

Well, that was a reason he darn sure hadn't expected to hear.

Gage tried to work it out. Did Ford disapprove of the baby's daddy? But he shook his head. Then, what the heck would that have to do with Lynette's and his safety?

Especially Gage's.

He moved closer, and met her eye to eye. "I'm missing something, and you're going to tell me what this pregnancy has to do with me."

Lynette swallowed hard, and her breath rushed out in a thin stream. "Gage, the baby is *yours.*"

Chapter Five

Lynette knew that telling Gage the truth could be a massive mistake. Everything at this point could be a wrong move for her, and she'd already made too many of those.

Maybe it was the shock of seeing him and learning he was alive. Maybe that spontaneous kiss of relief had melted her brain. And maybe it was this blasted attraction that just wouldn't die. Whatever the reason, she hadn't been able to stop herself from blurting out what would no doubt be a bombshell for him.

The baby she was carrying was his.

Gage stared at her as if she'd lost her mind, but it wasn't exactly shock she saw in his expression. More like total disbelief. "Lynette, I haven't had sex with you in ten years," he reminded her.

Yes, ten years, one month and four days.

Yet she still remembered every inch of his body. His touch. The things he said to her in those intimate moments. That made her one sick puppy.

Or something worse.

Lynette was afraid to put a label on that *something worse* but a one-man woman came to mind. Despite smothering all the good things she had once felt for him, the memories still haunted her.

"You want to explain to me how I could have gotten

you pregnant?" But he didn't give her time to answer. "Did someone come to you, someone pretending to be me?"

"No," she quickly assured him. "I'm pretty good at detecting the real Gage versus a fake one." And there was no way he could argue with that. She'd certainly found him out soon enough despite the disguise and the altered voice.

He huffed and made a circular motion with his hand to prompt her to continue with her explanation about the pregnancy. Lynette debated where she should start and decided to go with the beginning.

"When you were twenty-one and got Hodgkin's, we were already making plans to get married." She tried to keep her voice level. And failed. "The doctors in San Antonio told you the treatment could make you sterile. We'd talked about having kids down the road, so you stockpiled some semen."

She paused to give him time to absorb that.

He didn't absorb it well.

Gage cursed, a long string of profanity. "The hospital kept it after all this time?"

Lynette nodded. "Until about six weeks ago. When the hospital couldn't reach you, they called me because you'd listed me as your emergency contact. They wanted my permission to dispose of it since it'd been there so long. I, uh, took it instead."

There were few times that she could remember when Gage had been gobsmacked, and this was one of them.

He cursed again and scrubbed his hands over his face. "Why the heck would you do this?"

"Because I wanted a baby." *Your* baby—something else she kept to herself. In fact, there were other things she had to keep secret, as well.

Things that could make this situation even more dangerous than it already was.

"Plus, I thought you were dead," Lynette reminded him.

"Yeah, but my being dead wouldn't prevent the fallout from Ford if he found out the kid is mine."

"My father didn't know about the frozen sperm, and I had no plans to tell him. In fact, I don't intend to tell him about the baby, period. I'd planned to be out of Silver Creek before I started showing."

"And you thought he'd just let you leave?" Gage asked.

"No. But I've been making arrangements for a new identity in a place far away from here so I can raise this baby and have the life I always wanted."

"A life with my baby." He punched the steering wheel. "Lynette, I'm not exactly in any position to be a father."

"I know." She couldn't say that fast enough. "And I don't expect you to be."

Did she?

Well, she hadn't expected him to be because she'd thought he was dead. But now...

No.

She couldn't go there, either.

Gage wasn't really back in her life. He was just here to save her.

"All right," he said, and repeated it. "I need you to get on that plane and leave. I'll try to figure out who's after you and how to stop it."

That seemed like the goodbye she'd been expecting, and Lynette wanted to hang on to this moment just a little longer. "I could stay and help you."

"No deal." Another of Gage's sayings. In this case, he delivered it with a stubbornness that she had no trouble hearing.

Lynette opened her mouth to argue. She didn't want Gage shouldering all the danger. But then she thought of her unborn child. Their baby. If she stayed, the baby would also be in danger.

"You'll go," he insisted. He glanced at her stomach again to let her know they were on the same wavelength. "Who else knows the baby you're carrying is mine?"

"Just you and me."

"What about the doctor in San Antonio who contacted you?" he pressed.

She shook her head. "I didn't tell him I'd planned to be inseminated."

"No, but it isn't much of a stretch for him to figure it out. Someone could have followed you to the hospital and then paid off the doctor."

Another headshake. "I was careful, and I didn't have the insemination done there. I went to Houston, used a fake ID, and had it done at a private clinic where I paid to make sure my records would stay confidential."

He stared at her. "And all these precautions were because of your father?"

"Yes," she admitted, though she knew that would only lead to more questions.

It did.

Gage turned toward her. "Do you finally realize how dangerous a man he is?"

"Yes." Again, it would mean more questions. So, Lynette continued before Gage could ask them. "Ten years ago when my father found out we'd eloped, he said I had two choices. I could have the marriage annulled, or he'd kill you."

No profanity. No glare. But thanks to the lights on the runway, she could see his eyes, and the aha moment of truth. A truth she'd kept from him for a decade.

"And you believed him?" Gage pressed.

"Oh, yes." Lynette had to take a deep breath. "He convinced me after he confessed that he'd murdered my mother and gotten away with it."

There. She'd finally said it aloud. The words, the fear. The horrible secret she'd been carrying in her heart for so long that it was now part of her. Not just part of her past but her future.

Now, Gage cursed again. "You should have gone to Grayson. He could have arrested Ford."

"There was no evidence, just his confession that only I heard. He told me that before I could make it to the sheriff's office, you'd be dead and at least half your brothers, too." That required another deep breath. "I couldn't take the risk of losing you."

Ironic, since she'd lost him anyway.

Gage had hated her after the annulment. Still did. Well, maybe. He'd certainly responded to that kiss of relief. But Lynette couldn't pin her hopes on one kiss. Especially a kiss that could have been left over from the old heat between them. He could still lust after her without wanting anything to do with her.

"Ford wouldn't have killed me," Gage insisted.

"He convinced me otherwise." And that's all she could say for several seconds. "Remember, I disappeared for a week after we got married?"

"Oh, yeah. I remember. And that's when you told me you'd had the marriage annulled."

It was hard to deal with those old memories that were still so raw and painful, but Gage had to know. It might make him understand the danger. Not from men like Freddie Denton or Sampson Dalvetti. No, this danger was much closer.

"My father had me committed to an insane asylum in

Mexico," she explained, trying to sound clinical. "Let's just say it wasn't a fun place, and he did that to me to prove that he had complete control of me and my life."

Gage's mouth dropped open. "He put you in a crazy house?"

"He did. And he called me every day to remind me that he could keep me there while he murdered you." She stared at him. "Gage, he did that and didn't leave a paper trail or any trace of what he'd done."

He turned her to face him. "You should have told someone."

"I did! I told the authorities in Mexico, but my father had fake doctors' reports saying I was paranoid and needed to be institutionalized. He has a lot of power. A lot of friends in the right places to do whatever wrong he wants to do."

Gage didn't answer, but she could see his jaw muscles stirring. He let go of her and stared out at the rain and the runway.

"After I thought you were dead, I dug into those files because I was looking for some proof that he'd killed my mother," she continued. "I figured I could send him to jail for the rest of his life."

Gage shot her another glare. "If he sent you to the crazy house and killed your mother, then he'd kill you. It was too dangerous for you to go looking for proof that could put you in the grave."

"I know. And that's why I stopped after the doctor called from San Antonio."

Another aha flash went through his eyes.

"I quit looking for proof of my father's guilt because I wanted a baby. And I wanted to keep my baby safe."

"Clearly, you failed at that," he mumbled. "Why'd you use my sperm and not some anonymous donor from a sperm bank? That would have been a heck of a lot safer for you if your father found out."

She hesitated, carefully considering her answer. Gage probably wouldn't want to hear that the only baby she wanted was his. No. Not with everything that'd happened between them. Besides, it might make him feel as if she were trying to pressure him to coming back into her life.

"Going through a sperm bank would have added another step to the process," she settled for saying. "To keep my father from finding out, I would have had to create another identity to get a donor. It just seemed simpler to use what the doctor in San Antonio was offering me rather than go to another source."

Gage looked at her, and Lynette braced herself for the next set of questions. The ones where he would press for the truth about what she'd just told him. Or maybe he'd want to know how she felt about that decade-old annulment. She couldn't tell him that it'd crushed her. That it had left a wound inside her that would never heal.

No. Gage couldn't know that.

Because it would make him go after her father. Not with the cool head of a CIA operative, either. Gage would confront him in a hot moment of temper, and there would be one of two outcomes.

Gage would kill her father.

Or her father would kill him.

Without proof that her father had done the unspeakable crime of killing her mother, Gage would look guilty of killing an innocent man. One with lots of power and money. A man that Gage had let plenty of people know that he hated and would like to see dead.

The wave of nausea hit her so quickly that she hadn't felt it coming. Lynette took a deep breath. Several of them. It didn't help. She hadn't had a twinge of morning sickness, but maybe that's what this was. Or maybe she was just sick at the thought of never seeing Gage again.

But it was worth the price to keep him alive—especially now that he hadn't been killed eleven months ago.

Lynette buttoned her coat and reached for the door handle to open it. "Where are you sending me?" she asked.

He didn't answer right away. He continued to stare at her. "To a friend who's a federal marshal over in Maverick County. He'll keep you safe."

She hoped that was true. Hoped that safety was even possible at this point. "Will my father or another hit man be able to trace where the plane is going?"

"I'll take care of that," Gage promised. "I'll contact you when everything's been resolved."

She believed him. Well, she believed he would try anyway. "And you'll be careful?"

"Deal. Hey, I'm a careful guy," he added, splashing each word with his trademark drawl and cockiness.

Mercy, this was torture, knowing that Gage would have to face down a killer while she was tucked away in another county with a marshal.

Since there was nothing else to say that wouldn't get her in more trouble, Lynette just nodded and opened the door of the SUV. Gage did, too, on the driver's side. But before her foot even touched the ground, Gage caught on to her and yanked her back inside.

"What's wrong?" she asked.

He didn't get a chance to answer. In front of them, on the runway, the small plane burst into a ball of flames.

GAGE DIDN'T THINK about what had just happened. He went on autopilot, relying on his training and experience. The second he had Lynette on the seat, he threw the SUV into gear, slammed his foot on the accelerator and got them out of there.

Fast.

"The plane blew up," Lynette said. She wasn't just shaky. That was pure panic Gage heard in her voice. "The plane blew up." She just kept repeating it while she stared back at the ball of flames.

Yeah, it'd blown up all right. That meant they had an even bigger problem than he'd anticipated, and he had anticipated some pretty bad things.

"Why did it blow up?" she asked, the panic going up a notch.

"I'm not sure." But he had to find out. Somehow.

Gage glanced at the secure phone attached to the dash. It was supposed to be untraceable, but Gage couldn't take the risk that someone had managed to tap in to it. He also couldn't risk calling his handler, Sherman Hendricks. Sherman wasn't dirty. He was positive of that, but it didn't mean someone around Sherman hadn't discovered that Gage was still alive and betrayed him.

"Who did this?" Lynette asked. She still had her attention fastened to the rear window. Her eyes were wide, and she was shaking all over.

"I don't know that, either. Not yet. But put on your seat belt," Gage ordered.

With the slick, wet roads and the speed he was going, conditions were ripe for an accident. That was the last thing they needed if someone was already on their tails.

Lynette did put on her seat belt, though he didn't know how she managed with her hands shaking like crazy. "I was supposed to be on that plane."

Stating the obvious, but it was unnecessary to remind Gage of that, and he couldn't let *what could have been* distract him now. He got off the airport road and took the first side road he could.

"Did the pilot blow up the plane?" Lynette asked.

Possibly.

And that was another reason Gage couldn't call his handler. Sherman had also arranged for the pilot, who was a former operative. Hell. If they had a leak in communication or a mole, it was a really bad time for it. Gage needed backup and resources, and at the moment he was short on both of those.

"I'll get answers soon," Gage promised her. "But first, I have to get you someplace safe."

She shook her head. "Is that possible?" Her shaky voice hadn't calmed even a little. Probably because she'd had a double whammy of danger this morning.

"Eventually, I'll find somewhere for you to go." It would take some doing since he couldn't contact anyone in the CIA for help, not until he'd cleared up the possible leak issue.

"Oh, God." She dropped her head against the back of the seat and slid her hand over her stomach.

That shot a new round of alarm through him. "Are you okay? Are you having pains or something?"

It hit him then. She could lose the baby. She was only weeks into this pregnancy, and the trauma of all of this could cause her to miscarry.

That hit him even harder than the explosion.

Until minutes ago, Gage hadn't known about this baby. He darn sure hadn't planned it, either, but he would do everything within his power to keep Lynette and the child safe.

"No pains," she assured him. "I'm just scared for the baby and us."

So was he, but Gage kept that to himself. Lynette was

barely holding it together as it was, and she didn't need to know that he was shaking in his boots.

Oh, man.

He'd faced enemy fire and cold-blooded assassins, but that felt like Little League compared to this.

She glanced behind them again, but Gage already knew there wasn't anything to see now that the airport and flaming plane were out of sight. No one was following them, and to make sure it stayed that way, he rolled down his window and tossed out the secure phone.

"Just in case," he told Lynette.

"In case of *what?*" she asked.

He didn't intend to answer that, either. It wouldn't do her or the baby any good for him to go through all the nightmarish scenarios that could play out.

"Just in case," he repeated.

That obviously didn't ease any of her concerns, but it was a necessity. Now, the question was—what was the next step? Gage went through his options and discarded them as quickly as they came.

Until he got to the last one.

Hell.

It was the only one that made sense. But it wouldn't be easy. Still, he had to put his personal feelings and issues aside and consider what was best for Lynette.

Though it wouldn't be easy for her, either.

"Are we going back to my house?" she asked, taking him by his arm.

"No." Not a chance. That's exactly where he'd directed a CIA cleanup team to go. A team that might have dirty agents who could leak their location. He didn't want Lynette near the place.

Gage turned onto the main road, and almost immediately he saw the lights from the town. Silver Creek.

Home.

Where he wouldn't be welcome.

But hopefully Lynette would be. Well, maybe she would be after Gage explained some things.

"Where are you taking me?" she asked. The concern was rising again.

Not just in her but in Gage, too.

Because in a few minutes he would walk into the sheriff's office and face the brothers who thought he was dead.

Chapter Six

Ahead of them on the road, Lynette spotted lights from a squad car.

The blue flashes of light whipped through the darkness and the rain-streaked windshield. Someone, probably one of Gage's brothers, was no doubt responding to the explosion at the airport. Maybe they'd find something that would ultimately lead to an arrest.

Her father, Nicole or Patrick.

Any one of them could be behind this.

Any one of them could want her dead.

That was suddenly crystal clear to her. The hit man was proof of that. Ditto for the exploding plane. But while Patrick or Nicole could be the culprit, this felt like her father's doing. Not getting his pristine hands dirty but rather hiring someone to blow her to smithereens.

And he or the person responsible had nearly succeeded.

She was about to remind Gage that they should get as far away from this place as possible. But Gage slowed down and turned into a parking lot.

A familiar one.

She looked at Gage as if he'd lost his mind. "This is the sheriff's office," she pointed out.

"Yeah." And that's all he said.

She huffed. "But your family doesn't know you're

alive. Plus, there's the danger with the drug lord guy coming after them if he finds out you're not dead."

Another *yeah*. He parked, turned off the engine. "I'm aware of all of that. I also know that anything I do at this point is a risk." He paused. "But doing nothing could be an even bigger risk."

Maybe. But when she thought about that, she shook her head. "We could go to a city like Dallas or Houston and get lost in the crowd."

He looked at her, his head cocked to a familiar angle. "My brothers will protect you with their lives."

They probably wouldn't protect him though. There was bad blood because he'd left after the annulment and had had only minimal contact with them since. He'd turned his back on his family, and that wouldn't earn him a warm, fuzzy welcome.

Especially since he was riding in on the heels of danger.

"This is just so we can regroup," Gage explained. "We'll tell as few people as possible and then leave as quickly as we can."

Because they sure as heck didn't want the news to get back to Sampson Dalvetti. The problem was it was very difficult to keep secrets in a small town. Lynette had managed it so far with the pregnancy....

But she froze.

And remembered that her father was a devious man with all those resources to help him with his deviousness.

Oh, mercy.

If her father knew about the baby, then he could have been so enraged that he would have sent that hit man.

"Let's do this fast," Gage told her. "I don't want you out in the open any longer than necessary."

She didn't budge. "Let me go alone. And you can disappear again. It'll be safer for you."

"Yeah. But not safer for you. I'm not leaving you in a parking lot in the rain. Heck, I'm not leaving, period, until I know you're protected."

She tried to object, tried to make him understand this was a bad idea, but Gage didn't listen. He hurried from the SUV, took Lynette by the arm and he got her moving toward the back entrance of the sheriff's office. The second he had the door open, he shoved her inside and then stepped protectively in front of her.

The sound of the movement and door must have alerted someone because Lynette heard footsteps. A moment later, Gage's older brother Mason appeared in the hall.

She silently groaned. Mason wasn't the friendliest of the Ryland clan. In fact, he looked far more dangerous than the criminals he arrested as a Silver Creek deputy. Thankfully, they didn't cross paths a lot because Mason did the bulk of the work to run the family ranch.

Mason made a slight sound. Barely a reaction at all. "So, you're alive," he snarled.

Gage gave his usual "yeah."

Not much of a welcome-home outpouring. Unlike hers. She'd kissed Gage, for heaven's sake. Something that shouldn't have happened. The brothers stood there, staring at each other, and it seemed to her as if they had an entire discussion without saying a word.

Mason finally lifted his shoulder. "Anyone else know you're back from the grave?"

Gage shook his head. "Just Lynette and my handler." He stepped to the side so that Mason could see her. "It has to stay that way. Who else is here?"

"Just me. Grayson and Dade are on their way to the

airport to check out the explosion." Mason paused. "Did you have anything to do with that?"

"Indirectly," Gage admitted. "The pilot and plane were supposed to get Lynette away from here."

"Someone tried to kill me," she volunteered. "A hit man."

Mason's eyebrow swung up. "Who'd you piss off?"

She shook her head. "I'm not sure."

"There's a slim possibility it's connected to me," Gage admitted. "There's a good reason I let everyone believe I was dead."

"Who'd you piss off?" Mason repeated, directing it this time to Gage.

"The wrong person." Gage paused then mumbled something she didn't catch.

"What's wrong with your voice?" Mason asked.

"A failed attempt at a disguise. It'll wear off soon." Gage huffed. "I need to use your phone. A landline."

Mason hitched his thumb to the office behind him. "Anything else?"

"Watch Lynette for me. Don't let her out of your sight."

As if he knew his order would be obeyed and obeyed well, Gage walked past his brother and disappeared into the office. Mason looked at her, at her wet dress, coat and hair.

"You knew he was alive?" Mason's question had an edge to it. But then, Mason always seemed to have an edge.

"No. Not until about an hour ago when he broke in to my house." It seemed like an eternity since that'd happened. Her entire world had been turned upside down in that hour, and she suspected Mason was feeling some of that, too.

Mason studied her, as if checking for some clues in her body language. "So, what's going on?"

She wearily shook her head. "We're not sure. A drug lord threatened to kill all of you. And me. That's why Gage faked his death. He figured if the drug lord thought he was dead, there'd be no reason to come after us."

"That's Gage. Always too stubborn to ask for help. Well, until now. But I suspect his help-asking has more to do with you than him." Mason studied her some more. "Are you two back together or what?"

"No." And she couldn't answer fast enough. Lynette even hiked up her chin and tried not to show any doubts. "Gage got word of the hit man, and he came to save me. That's all. I was supposed to get on that plane, leave and go to safety so that he could get out of here, too. But someone blew it up and messed up those plans."

Mason stayed quiet a moment. "So, what now? Gage just leaves again and pretends to be dead?"

Lynette hated the thought of it. Seeing him even for this short time had reopened all the old wounds that had never fully closed. Never would.

But yes, that's what had to happen.

Mason pulled in a long breath and motioned for her to follow him. She did and didn't bother to ask where he was taking her. He led her down the hall to the bathroom and pulled out a handful of paper towels.

"Thanks." She wiped her face and clamped onto her bottom lip when another wave of nausea hit her. Lynette slapped her hand on the wall to keep from staggering.

"You okay?" And there was so much concern in Mason's voice that Lynette forced herself to give him a quick nod.

"Fine," she lied.

He just kept staring her, and when his gaze dropped

to her stomach, Lynette thought she might panic. Mercy, was he suspicious that she might be pregnant? He couldn't be, because this was a man who could definitely put one and one together and come up with the correct answer.

Fortunately, Gage saved the moment, again. He came out of Mason's office and into the hall with them.

"The pilot's alive," Gage told them. "But other than that, we don't know anything else about the explosion."

"We?" Mason challenged.

"We," Gage repeated but he didn't clarify. He looked at her. "Are you okay?"

"Yes," she snapped.

At the same moment, Mason said, "She looks like she's about to throw up."

"It's been a rough morning," she added in a mumble and shot them both a *back off* stare. She didn't need any more questions about her or her sudden queasiness.

Gage flexed his eyebrows and thankfully moved on. Maybe because he understood it wouldn't help matters if Mason figured out she was pregnant. "I'm making arrangements for you to leave for a safe house."

"Hope it's safer than the plane was," Mason growled.

"It will be," Gage promised. "In the meantime, can she stay here?"

"Of course," Mason said without hesitation. "You'll stay, too?"

Gage shook his head. "Best if I work behind the scenes."

That earned him one of the Mason's infamous scowls. "In other words, you want me to lie and not tell the others you're alive."

"For now." Gage's attention went from his brother and back to her. But he didn't get a chance to tell her whatever he was about to say because the bell over the front door jingled.

The bell meant they had a visitor.

Gage didn't wait in the hall to see who'd just come in. He ducked back inside Mason's office and slapped off the lights before he peered around the doorjamb to get a look at who had just entered the sheriff's building.

Mason cursed, and for a moment Lynette thought the profanity was for Gage's response or maybe even this whole mess of a situation. But then she followed Mason's gaze toward the front of the sheriff's office.

And to the two people who'd just stepped inside.

No. Not this. Not now. Their timing couldn't have possibly been any worse.

Lynette saw Nicole Manning, her father's longtime girlfriend, campaign manager and business associate.

However, Nicole wasn't alone.

Senator Ford Herrington nailed his gaze to Lynette and made a beeline down the hall toward her. Toward Mason. And toward Gage.

Oh, God.

Lynette tried to brace herself for the worst.

GAGE HADN'T THOUGHT this morning could possibly get any more complicated, but he'd obviously been wrong.

Two of their suspects had just walked into the sheriff's station, and there was no time to get Lynette or himself out of there.

Lynette shot him a *stay put* glare. Mason, too. And then his brother thankfully stepped in front of Lynette. Mason also drew his gun, and while Gage couldn't see Nicole's and Ford's reactions, he'd bet his favorite snakeskin boots that they weren't good ones.

"The firearm isn't called for, Deputy," Ford grumbled

in that high-class ice-cold voice of his. And Gage hadn't missed the demeaning way he'd referred to Mason as a *deputy.* In Ford's mind that was one step below hoof grit. His opinion of Gage was even lower than that.

Maybe his opinion of Lynette, too.

Gage wished the man would give Mason and him an excuse to shoot first and ask questions later. But then he rethought that. It was the last thing he wanted to happen because Lynette would be in the line of fire again.

Two attempts on her life were enough.

Besides, Ford was too smooth to pick a fight with witnesses around. No. For him, it was all about appearances. A perfect public image reserved for everyone but his enemies. He was probably planning to send Lynette back to the crazy house in Mexico.

"Lynette, you're here," Nicole said. No ice for her. The woman sounded concerned, but Gage knew that could be faked. After all, Nicole slept with Ford on a regular basis, and she'd no doubt learned some of his tricks.

"She is here," Mason verified. "But the real question is—why are *you* here?"

Gage smiled. No one had ever accused Mason of being a nice guy, and he gave them back as much snark as Ford had doled out to him.

"I called my daughter's house," Ford calmly explained, "and when she didn't answer, Nicole and I drove over to check on her."

"We were worried," Nicole added. "Especially when we saw that someone had broken your bedroom window."

Broken, not shot. Of course, maybe Ford knew the difference, especially if he'd been the one to send the hit man who'd shot through that glass.

"Someone tried to kill me," Lynette said.

Oh, man. She sounded shaky, and he hated she had to

go through this. If Gage had thought for one second that revealing himself would make this better, he'd be out in that hall with them.

But it wouldn't make things better.

It might spur on her father or someone else to try to kill her again. Right here, right now. After all, he was betting that Nicole was carrying a weapon in that purse that he'd managed to get just a glimpse of before he'd had to duck into the office and out of sight.

"Any idea who'd try to kill Lynette?" Mason asked. He still didn't ease up on the snide tone, and he asked it in such a way to let them know that he not only knew the answer, they *were* the answer.

"No," Ford and Nicole said in unison.

"Why would we?" Ford continued.

Mason shrugged. "I figured you must have suspected Lynette was in some kind of danger. I mean, why else would you call her at such an early hour and then have driven over there in this storm?"

Gage heard Ford step closer, and he ducked deeper into the dark office. "Is that an accusation?" Ford challenged.

"It's a question," Mason clarified. "A simple one. I was kind of hoping for a simple response."

The seconds crawled by.

"I was worried about her," Ford spoke up. The facade was back in place now, and he sounded like a concerned daddy. "I'd tried to talk to Lynette yesterday, and she seemed frazzled, or something."

"It was the *or something,*" Lynette answered. "I was busy at work and didn't have time for your call. Besides, I didn't want to talk to you."

Gage smiled again. Lynette really had developed some sass when it came to her father. Too bad it had come ten years too late.

"Why did you try to call me this morning?" Lynette pressed. "And why bring Nicole in on this? I don't trust her, and I don't want her or you doing welfare checks on me."

"So, now you're accusing me?" Nicole snarled. "You'd better think before you speak."

"I have," Lynette assured her. "I think about you a lot. My father and Patrick, too. And what I'd like is for you both to leave. If you aren't going to tell us why you're really here, then you're of no help."

But Gage didn't hear anybody jumping to leave.

"Who tried to kill you?" Ford asked. He took down his tone a notch.

Now, there was movement. Lynette stepped closer to her father, and Gage silently cursed. He didn't want her closer. He wanted her tucked safely behind Mason and his gun.

"He didn't tell me his name," Lynette simply stated. "He just shot and ran."

That was partly true. The hit man had indeed run—after Lynette and him.

"So, it could have been a botched burglary attempt," Nicole suggested after blowing out what sounded to be a breath of relief.

"Could be," Lynette agreed, but there was no agreement in her voice. Lynette stared at the woman so long that Gage had to wonder what had snagged her attention.

"There," Nicole concluded. "The mystery's solved, and the sheriff can start looking for a burglar. Maybe it was a kid who got scared when he realized you were home."

"Maybe." But there was still no hint of agreement. "Now, if you don't mind, Mason here has to take my statement, and I have to fill out an insurance claim for the broken window. Then I'd like to get some sleep. Nearly getting killed has made me a little cranky."

Gage saw Ford's hand snake out, and for one horrifying moment Gage thought this was all about to come to a head with Mason pulling his gun. And both men firing. But Ford only aimed his finger at her.

"You need to be careful," Ford warned. It didn't exactly sound fatherly, but the words were right. He added, "Call me after you've had time to rest."

"Of course," Lynette replied. Again, there was no hint of cooperation in her voice. Just the opposite.

Gage finally heard the sounds he wanted to hear. Footsteps. Followed by the bell jangling over the door. He was ready to step out when Mason motioned for him to stay put.

"Anything else, Nicole?" Lynette asked.

So, the woman hadn't left with Ford after all. Why? But Gage figured he'd soon hear the answer.

"Your father's under a lot of stress," Nicole finally said. "You need to cut him some slack."

"Why would I do that?" Lynette snapped, and she folded her arms over her chest.

Even though Gage couldn't see Nicole's face or expression, neither Mason nor Lynette seemed pleased with her presence or this waffling conversation.

"Ford makes it hard on everyone when he's under stress," Nicole added. "Especially on me."

Lynette made a sound of weary amusement. "I doubt he's been any harder on you than he has on me. You know what he's capable of, and yet you still go to his bed. If you're looking for sympathy, you won't get it from me."

"It's not sympathy," Nicole said, her voice quivering on the last word. "It's self-preservation. For all our sakes, Lynette, back off."

Gage heard more footsteps, and the bell jangled again.

"She's gone," Mason told him. "Now, would both of you mind explaining to me what the heck is going on?"

Gage walked to the doorway and tried to assemble an explanation that would be short, sweet and effective. "Someone hired a hit man to come after Lynette. I suspect it's because she was trying to learn some things about her father and his business associates. Nicole, included. That's why Nicole's running scared and gave that cryptic warning."

Mason swung his attention to her. "Does this have to do with your mother's death?"

"Maybe," she admitted, and she seemed surprised that Mason zoomed right in on that. "My father told me he killed her, and I was looking for proof."

Mason cursed. "You should have come to Grayson or me with this."

"Too dangerous." Lynette said, then paused. "My father's a dangerous man."

"Never doubted it for a minute," Mason said. He looked back at Gage. "So, Ford sent this hit man because Lynette figured out the truth?"

Gage had to shake his head. "It could have been Nicole."

"Yes," Lynette verified.

Gage remembered the look Lynette had given the woman. "Did you see something that made you more suspicious?"

Lynette stayed quiet a moment. "Something wasn't right, but I'm not sure what. It was almost as if Nicole was scared. Not just of me but my father."

"She's not usually scared of him?" Mason pressed.

"No," Lynette answered. "Nicole has a warped sense of right and wrong when it comes to my father, and she could have done this to protect him. Plus, she's no doubt had some dirty dealings of her own, and maybe I got too close to learning the truth about her."

"What about Ford's business partner, Patrick Harkin?" Mason asked.

"Also a suspect," Gage answered. Mason clearly understood the dynamics of what was going on here. No surprise though. He'd been a deputy sheriff for fifteen years, and there wasn't much that went on that Mason didn't know about.

"I stopped my investigation," Lynette told his brother. "But I might have stopped too late."

Mason gave a weary sigh. "Or this could have come from that drug lord you mentioned." He looked at Gage for verification.

And Gage couldn't deny it. There was only a slim chance that Sampson Dalvetti had done this, but he couldn't rule it out completely.

This time Mason huffed. "So, what's the plan? I don't want to face a drug lord or Ford and his crew unless we have something worked out."

Gage had already been going over this in his head, but the devil was in the details. The possible danger, too. "I need Lynette in protective custody until I can get this safe house nailed down. And I also have to disappear while I do that. Deal?"

Judging from the look on Mason's face, he was about to disagree with some part of the plan. But he didn't have time to voice that argument.

The back door flew open.

So fast that Gage barely had time to react. He took hold of Lynette, dragged her behind him and drew his gun.

Chapter Seven

Lynette had tried to prepare herself for the worst—another hit man—but it was Gage's brother Grayson who came through the door. Grayson's attention went straight to Gage, and he stopped cold.

"Yeah, he's alive," Mason announced. No emotion in his voice. Unlike Grayson's face.

There were a lot of emotions there, including shock and anger. Those came first, but then Lynette saw something else. Something stronger. Relief.

Maybe.

Grayson hurried up the hall, grabbed on to Gage and hugged him. Okay. She could breathe a little easier. It had been relief, and Lynette knew exactly how Grayson felt. Gage's eldest brother had been more of a father than a sibling.

"I could beat you to pulp for letting us believe you were dead," Grayson told him.

"I didn't have a choice," Gage whispered. He pulled back and met Grayson's gaze. "Still don't. I'll explain it all later, once Lynette is safe."

Grayson looked at Lynette. Then, at Gage again. "Are you two back together?"

"No," Lynette assured him, but since Mason had asked her the same darn question just minutes earlier she wondered just how obvious the heat was that was still zinging between Gage and her.

Heat that had to end.

She hoped reminding herself of that would work.

Gage wearily scrubbed his hand over his face. "Look, I know I don't have a right to ask, but I need you and Mason to keep Lynette safe while I do some things."

She grabbed Gage's arm. "Things that don't involve my father, right?"

"Things that involve your safety," he answered. Which wasn't at all an answer to her question. He looked at his brothers. "The plane that blew up was supposed to get Lynette out of here."

Grayson shook his head. "The fire chief thinks the explosion wasn't an accident."

She didn't believe it had been, and Lynette was having a hard time getting past the fact that she'd been within just seconds from death.

Grayson turned his attention to Mason. "Why don't you go ahead and take Lynette to the ranch?"

"The ranch?" Gage challenged. "It's not safe enough."

"Oh, these days the ranch is plenty safe," Mason assured him. "We've had some trouble over the past couple of months so we increased security. Plus, all my ranch hands know how to shoot."

Lynette knew all about the trouble. There'd been several attempts to break in to the place and even some shootings. But the talk of the town was that the ranch had become more like a fortress. That was partly because all five of Gage's brothers lived there, and they were all in law enforcement. So was one spouse, and another spouse was the assistant district attorney.

"A lot has changed since you've been gone," Grayson

continued. He held up his left hand to show Gage the wedding band that was there.

"I heard." Gage shrugged. "I had my handler keep tabs on all of you. You and Eve are married with a baby on the way. I'm happy for you both. You and Eve belong together."

"Funny," Grayson commented. "We always said that about Lynette and you."

"Yeah, funny," Gage grumbled.

The silence was long and awkward. Lynette didn't volunteer anything. She'd already blabbed enough for one night. If she'd kept her mouth shut about the baby, she might have been able to talk Gage into leaving. Into going someplace safe.

But she doubted she could do that now.

She hadn't been sure of what Gage's reaction would be to her pregnancy, though she had thought about it. Actually, she'd thought about every possible aspect considering Gage. That he was alive. That he would return. But none of the fantasies involved him risking his life to save her.

"Can you take Lynette to the ranch now?" Gage asked Mason.

Mason nodded, but Lynette didn't budge. "I need a moment alone with Gage," she insisted.

Grayson exchanged glances with Mason, and they started up the hall toward the front dispatch desk to give Gage and her some privacy.

"What are you going to do?" Lynette came right out and asked.

He lifted his shoulder as if the answer were obvious. It wasn't, and she let him know that with a scowl.

"Safe house preparations," he clarified. "I need to get a report on the explosion and the hit man cleanup."

She waited for more, much more, but that's all he

said. "Will I see you again?" Lynette hated that her voice cracked and tears burned in her eyes.

Great. Nothing like a sobbing hormonal woman for Gage's send-off into what would no doubt be a life-and-death situation. She didn't think for a minute that Gage was only going to do those two things he'd named.

Lynette waved Gage off when he started to pull her into his arms. "I can stand on my own two feet," she reminded him.

And herself.

In fact, she'd spent years trying to overcome the fear that her father had put inside her.

Lynette cursed the tears that came anyway.

"Right now, you look like you're about to fall off your own two feet," Gage whispered, and put his arms around her despite her protest. "No shame in that. You're tired, cold, and you've been through two sets of trouble already, and the sun hasn't even come up."

"Three sets," Lynette corrected. "You didn't include yourself."

"Yeah," he mumbled. He pushed her still wet hair away from her face and used the pad of his thumb to swipe off the tear that streaked down her cheek. "I always was trouble for you."

Trouble in a body that still heated her up in one second and infuriated in the next.

That was Gage.

Their relationship had never been easy.

"You should come with a warning label attached," she whispered. "Especially one attached to the zipper of your jeans." That part of him was just as much trouble for her as the rest of him. Maybe more.

"Oh, yeah? What should that warning label say?"

Amusement danced through his eyes while the Texas drawl danced off his words.

She could think of a few. *Caution: Hot.* Or maybe *Danger Ahead.*

"Do not remove," she settled for saying and hoped that the joke would lighten the mood.

It didn't.

"Will I see you again?" she repeated, fearing a no and a yes equally. Either one would be yet another complication.

"Afraid so." He brushed a kiss on her cheek. It was a peck but not chaste.

Gage's mouth was never chaste.

Their gazes met, and he was so close that Lynette could give him a real kiss. Like the one in the SUV. And she thought about it, she really did, especially since his *afraid so* could be a lie. This might be the last time she saw him again.

Lynette stared at him, trying to remember every detail in case this was indeed the last time. His dark brown hair was a little too long as usual. Gage always managed to look like a rock star who'd just climbed out of bed. Rumpled. Kissable. Hot.

But one of the details was wrong.

"Your eyes," she mumbled.

"Colored contacts." He touched his index finger to first his left eye and then his right. No more brown.

Lynette smiled at the gunmetal-gray eyes that stared back at her. "Killer eyes, I used to call them."

"How romantic. Guys like to hear that kind of talk from a woman." But he smiled, too.

Her smile faded just as quickly. Killer as in they always did her in. Those eyes still worked magic on her. And that couldn't happen. Even though it would rip her heart apart again, it was best to let Gage go.

But maybe she could risk a goodbye kiss.

"We've got company," Grayson called back to them.

It broke the kissing urge in a snap, and Gage stepped into the first office he reached, and as he'd done before, he turned off the lights.

Good thing, because Patrick Harkin entered the building.

"Lucky us," Lynette mumbled. "Patrick is here."

Gage groaned, and Lynette agreed. She was too tired for another round with another suspect. But she doubted she could avoid it completely. Her best bet was just to make it as short as possible.

"I heard about the explosion at the airport," Patrick greeted. "I wanted to find out what happened."

Maybe it was an honest question, but when Patrick looked at her, something inside her snapped. No more need to make this short. She was riled enough to ask questions and force the answers out of him.

"Did you hire someone to try to kill me?" Lynette demanded.

Gage groaned again, and she went up the hall so that he wouldn't have a chance to grab her and pull her into the room with him. She was tired of playing the whiny victim here. She wasn't helpless, and Patrick was about to learn that the hard way.

"I have no idea what you're talking about." Patrick's tone suddenly didn't seem so casual. "Nicole called me and said a burglar tried to break in to your house."

"Not a burglar. And he didn't try to break in. He fired shots into my bedroom window and tried to murder me."

Patrick looked appropriately shocked. "I had nothing to do with that."

"Didn't you?" she pressed. She went closer, hoping to violate his personal space and then some. "Because I don't trust you, and I think you have plenty to hide." Lynette went even closer. "But here's the bottom line, Patrick. This stops now. Hear me? *Now!*"

He shook his head, as if ready to deny that, but Lynette waved him off. "I'm thinking anything you say right now will be a lie so just save your breath."

Mason stepped to her side. "So, did you hire a nut job to kill Lynette?"

Lynette knew Mason was far more intimidating than she was. It felt good to have someone on her side again, and it didn't feel as if she were leaning on him. Just the opposite. She'd missed this camaraderie with Gage's family.

"No, absolutely not," Patrick insisted. His expression morphed from surprised to indignant concern. "I'm a businessman, for Pete's sake. Besides, I don't have a reason to kill her or anyone else."

"Yes, you do," Lynette corrected. "At least you think you have one, but when I was doing all that snooping around, I didn't find anything that implicates you in a crime."

"I'm still looking," Mason added. "In fact, this little visit just makes me want to dig harder to see what's put that fear in your beady little eyes."

Patrick's face turned bright red, and it seemed to take him several seconds to put his temper in check. He turned his narrowed gaze to Grayson. "You need to call off your brother, or you could find the sheriff's office slapped with a lawsuit for slander."

Grayson shrugged. "It's not slander if it's true." He casually checked his watch. "Tell you what—it's barely 6:00 a.m. Too early for an interrogation since I haven't even had my coffee yet. But come back at 8:00. We'll talk then. Or rather, you'll talk, and I'll listen."

"Is that an order?" Patrick demanded.

"Yes, it is," Grayson answered, and Lynette nearly cheered.

"Fine," Patrick spit out. "I'll be here, but I'm bringing my lawyers." He stormed out, slamming the door behind so hard that the bell clattered to the floor.

"I'll send you a bill for that," Mason called.

They stood there long enough to make sure Patrick wasn't going to come rushing back in.

"I'll get Ford and Nicole in here at the same time so Dade and I can interrogate them all at once," Grayson explained. "With their tempers, one of them might blow up and say something incriminating."

"Don't count on it," Lynette mumbled. "Especially from my father. His sheep's clothing hides the wolf very well in public. Besides, his lawyers aren't going to let him speak."

Another shrug from Grayson. "Maybe one of the other two will rattle, then." He looked at Mason. "Go ahead and take Lynette to the ranch."

It was time. Gage and she had technically already said their goodbyes, and now she somehow had to make it out of there without crying.

Mason and she started down the hall, and Gage stepped out. He gave her a look. That's all. No words. But he followed them into the parking lot.

The sun hadn't come up yet, so they only had the overhead security lights. Mason paused in the doorway and glanced around, his attention swinging from one side of the parking lot to the other. He also put his hand over the gun in his shoulder holster before he led her straight toward a cruiser that was parked next to Gage's SUV.

She looked over her shoulder to get one last look at Gage, but the sound stopped her cold. It was barely a sound at all, more like some movement that she caught from the corner of her eye.

"Get down!" Mason shouted.

He didn't wait for her to respond. He grabbed her and pulled her to the side of the cruiser.

Just like that, Lynette's heart was in her throat again, and the fear returned. The questions, too.

What was going on now?

Other than the possible movement, Lynette hadn't seen anyone in the parking lot, but Mason and Gage apparently had.

Both had their weapons drawn.

She followed Mason's gaze to the front part of the parking lot. Toward the street. More specifically, toward the hardware store directly across from the sheriff's office. There was a thin alley there, pitch-black, and she didn't have to be a lawman to realize it would be the perfect place for a hit man to hide.

But was it another hit man?

They waited for what seemed an eternity with her fears rising and with their attention locked on that alley. Mason didn't move a muscle, and from what she could see of Gage, neither did he.

Lynette was on the verge of deciding this was all a false alarm when there was another sound. Not movement this time. It happened fast, a zinging sound ripping through the air, and something slammed into the SUV.

"A shot," Mason mumbled along with some profanity.

Oh, God. Her heart dropped again. It hadn't been a regular blast— She'd already heard her share of those this morning. This one sounded as if it'd come from a gun rigged with a silencer. And she knew that couldn't be good. Someone was trying to kill them and trying not to be heard. Probably so that the sheriff and any deputies inside wouldn't come running.

The gunman ran though. He came out of the alley, sending a stream of shots their way. Nonstop. The bullets pelted into the SUV and the concrete surface of the parking lot. Mason shoved her lower to the ground and crawled over her back. Protecting her. Just as Gage had done in the woods when Denton was firing at them.

Lynette caught just a glimpse of the gunman as he darted out of the alley and disappeared from her line of sight. But apparently not from Mason's.

"He's at your six o'clock," Mason yelled to Gage.

"I got him," Gage answered.

Lynette tried to pick through the darkness and the rain to see the threat, but Gage apparently had already located whatever or whoever was out there.

Gage took aim.

Fired.

Since his gun didn't have a silencer, the two shots blasted through the parking lot.

And then nothing.

Everything seemed to freeze. Except her heartbeat. It was pounding so hard that Lynette thought her ribs might crack.

Even though Mason was practically all over her, Lynette could see Gage from beneath Mason's cover. With his weapon ready and aimed, Gage took slow, cautious steps toward the street. Lynette saw it then.

The man on the ground.

She pulled in her breath. Held it. And prayed that the guy didn't get up and start firing again. But he didn't move. Gage made his way to him, stooped down and touched his fingers to his neck.

"Dead," he relayed to Mason.

Mason stood, and somehow so did she. It was the second time today she'd seen a dead man, and it didn't get easier. She was thankful for that. Thankful, too, that Gage had managed to save her once again.

But this couldn't continue. Sooner or later, a gunman might get lucky, and it could cost them everything—including their lives. It was bad enough that she was in danger, but now she'd brought that danger to his family. Maybe to the entire town, because anyone nearby could have been shot with a stray bullet.

"You know who he is?" Mason asked.

Gage nodded and quickly made his way back to Lynette. "His name is Walter Jonavich. He's a hit man who often pairs up with Freddie Denton, the guy who tried to kill Lynette earlier."

Oh, mercy. She used the cruiser to steady herself. "You don't think Denton brought along someone else, do you?" she managed to ask.

But Gage didn't answer her, which was an answer in itself. And that answer was *yes.* Then Gage got her moving.

"I'll call for a cleanup," Gage told his brother. He headed straight for one of the cruisers. "But I'm getting Lynette out of here *now.*"

Chapter Eight

Gage pulled the cruiser to a stop directly in front of the guesthouse on the Ryland ranch. The main house was much larger and just a quarter of a mile away, but he'd decided against taking Lynette there. According to his conversation with Grayson, the guesthouse and the grounds around it were equally safe.

And this way, Lynette and he wouldn't have to deal with the rest of his family.

Well, not yet anyway.

Eventually he would have to decide how to handle all of this—the danger and his so-called homecoming—but for now he just wanted to get Lynette inside, so she could get her mind off the fact that she'd nearly been killed. Again.

Gage should have anticipated that Denton wouldn't come alone. But he'd screwed it up. In hindsight while Denton was at Lynette's house, his sidekick, Walter Jonavich, probably had been at the airport putting an explosive device on the plane. Of course, one of their other suspects could have done that, too, but the bottom line was that someone had known that Lynette was supposed to be at the airport and on that plane.

And it was that someone who clearly wanted her dead.

"How long will we stay here at the guesthouse?" Lynette asked, pulling his attention back to her.

"A day at the most. We'll leave as soon as the safe house is ready."

She nodded. "Thanks," Lynette added when he opened the passenger's side door to help her out. She stood, looked up at him and met his gaze. "But you can get that worried look off your face. I'm fine. The baby's fine."

"Yeah, because we got lucky." And Gage would never forget that something as fragile as luck had played into this.

"No. Because you're a good shot."

She gave his arm a friendly pat and walked ahead of him and into the single-story cottage-style guesthouse. Everything about it looked homey, from its fresh white exterior to its porch complete with a swing and rocking chairs. Heck, it even had a picket fence and flower beds.

It was a place with fond memories.

It'd once been his grandfather's house, and after he had been killed twenty years ago, the family had used it for guests and for the occasional ranch hand or two before Mason had built a massive bunkhouse to accommodate the workers.

But years ago, this house had served a different purpose. When Lynette was seventeen, Gage had sneaked her in so they could have sex for the first time. Over the next two years, they'd come back. For more sex and some heavy-duty make out sessions.

It'd happened so often Gage used to get aroused just driving past the place.

Lynette looked back at him, the corner of her mouth lifting as if she knew what he was thinking. "It's been a while," she mumbled.

A while that seemed like yesterday. It was way too

fresh in his mind, and especially his body, and Gage started to wonder if this might be as big a mistake as his plan that'd already backfired.

Still, he didn't stuff her back in the cruiser and drive away. Like a moth to a flame he followed Lynette past the gate and into the yard.

"Bittersweet," she added, and paused on the bottom step so she could take the place in.

Oh, yeah. It was exactly that.

"You cried after the first time," he reminded her. That, too, was a darn fresh memory for something that'd happened fourteen years ago.

She made a sound of agreement, went up the steps and opened the front door. "Because I thought you wouldn't respect me."

Surprised, Gage shook his head. It was the first time he'd heard an explanation for those tears.

He followed her into the living room and shut the door. Gage also armed the newly installed security system that Mason had told him about. "I never did understand that logic. Did you lose respect for me?"

"Never," she mumbled.

At least that's what he thought she said.

Never meant a lot to him, considering all the crap that had happened after their so-called marriage. Of course, he'd probably misunderstood her.

She took off her shoes, which were caked with mud from their run through the woods. "I need to grab a shower."

Good idea. Anything to help her relax. And it might help if he had her out of his sight for a moment or two so he could get his bearings. He felt off-kilter, and it wasn't a good time for that. Best to keep his mind on the assignment of protecting Lynette rather than taking arousing trips down memory lane.

"After your shower, you should eat something," Gage added. "Mason said he had one of the ranch hands stock the fridge for us."

Lynette nodded.

Gage nodded.

But she didn't move.

Neither did Gage, though he knew he darn well should be hoofing it out of there, away from her and away from the stupid mistake he was thinking about making.

Lynette glanced into the open door of the bedroom. And at the bed where she'd lost her virginity to him. It was covered with the same patchwork quilt.

Then, she glanced at him, as if waiting for something. "I can *feel* the memories here," she whispered.

So could he. He could feel them in every part of his body. Especially the parts involved in creating those memories that they still felt.

She turned, just a little, and he saw her breasts rise and fall with her suddenly shallow breath. Lynette probably didn't know it, but she was sending out a signal that his body had no trouble interpreting.

She ran her tongue over her bottom lip.

Okay, so maybe she did know about the signal-sending. Maybe she wanted exactly what he wanted. Being on the same page could be a good thing. Or bad.

Really bad.

That still didn't stop him.

Forcing any of those *really bad* doubts aside, Gage went to her, and in the same motion he hauled her into his arms.

"What are you doing?" she asked. Her voice was all

breath and filled with more of those signals that yelled for him to take her now.

So, that's what Gage did.

"I'm dealing with what you started earlier in the SUV," he let her know.

Yeah, it was stupid to finish something that would only lead to more stupidity, but Gage was about a mile beyond being able to put on the brakes.

He put his mouth to hers and kissed her.

There was a lot of emotion built up inside him. He hadn't realized just how much. But he had realized, too many times to count, what Lynette did to him. Not just to his mouth. But to his entire body and mind.

She didn't stop him. She kissed him as if this was the first and last kiss she'd ever have. It was always like that with them. Life and death. Now or never.

Especially the *now* part.

The kiss fired up an urgency that Gage hadn't felt, well, since the last time they'd had one of these fiery kissing sessions. And he decided—what the heck. He might as well do this right.

He put her back against the wall so he could run his hands down her body. First her sides, then her breasts. Touching her made him crazy, but Lynette upped the ante by grinding her body against his. Sex to sex.

The woman knew how to make him crazy, too.

"We shouldn't be doing this," Lynette mumbled and then coiled her arms around him and dived back in for kissing, round three.

Gage couldn't agree more. They shouldn't be doing this. They had way too much to do than to be French-kissing against the wall.

That still didn't stop him.

But another thought at least caused him to slow down. "Are you okay? I mean, will this hurt the baby?"

She shook her head. "It won't hurt the baby," she assured him.

The words had barely left her mouth when Lynette pulled him back to her for another kiss. And Gage knew things were going to get way out of hand, especially after he shoved up her dress and located the flimsy lace panel on the front of her panties.

She went limp, the opposite of his reaction, and she made a sound mixed with both immense pleasure and hesitation. Yep, even through the fiery haze in his head and body, he heard the hesitation.

Gage pulled back a little, but he kept his hand in place. He touched her with his fingers through the lace.

"We have to think this through," she said. It would have been a good suggestion if she hadn't sounded on the verge of a climax and if she hadn't moved against his fingers, seeking his touch. "My head's not on straight right now."

Nothing was straight, he wanted to tell her.

Gage kept touching her, and he watched her eyelids flutter down. She made that sound again. The sound that heated every inch of his body that wasn't already scalding hot.

"You're a really good kisser, and I haven't had sex in a long time." She punctuated that with a breathy moan and ground her body against his fingers.

He touched her again. Kissed her, too.

Then stopped.

"How long of a time?" he risked asking.

She looked at him, but Gage caused her eyes to haze over again by sliding his hand into her panties and touching her the way he wanted. Naked skin to naked skin.

Judging from her reaction, she wanted it, too. So Gage slid his fingers into that wet, slick heat.

"Ten years," she whispered.

He was so caught up in sending her straight to a slippery climax that it took a few seconds for that to register. It didn't register well.

"Ten years?" he repeated. Gage stopped touching her.

But Lynette put his hand right back where it'd been.

"Don't read anything into it," she grumbled.

"Ten years as in when we were together?" he pressed. "That was the last time you had sex?"

She didn't answer verbally, but everything about her face and body language said *yes*.

"Oh, man." He paused. "Oh, man!" And that was all Gage could get out for several moments. "How the hell could I not read anything into that?" he asked. "Am I the only man you've ever been with?"

Lynette tried to move away from him, but Gage held her in place. Probably not the brightest idea he'd ever had with his erection between them.

"Don't read anything into it," she repeated. "It just took me a long time to get over you, that's all."

He looked at her face, flushed with arousal, her nipples that were drawn tight and puckered against her flimsy white lace bra. And her swollen lips from their kissing assault. She looked like sex. Smelled like it, too. And it was crystal clear what she wanted him to do.

"But you got over me?" he challenged.

She looked him straight in the eyes. "I did."

A different set of emotions roared through him. Bad ones that sent his blood boiling in a different way. "Tell me that lie again, Lynette, and I'll strip off those panties and take you where you stand. I'll be gentle with you because of the baby, but I *will* take you."

Her chin came up. "It's true. I got over you."

He might have believed her. If she hadn't made that hot shivery sound when his breath hit against her mouth.

Gage stared at her, sizing her up as he'd done with the enemy. But she wasn't the enemy. She was his ex-wife, and no matter what she said, Lynette hadn't gotten over him.

Hell.

There was no way he could ignore that. No way to stop without doing something to finish this.

He'd already broken all the rules anyway.

So, Gage slid his hand down her belly and back into her panties. He didn't kiss her, because he wanted to see her eyes. And he wanted her to see him.

For starters. He touched her. He'd given Lynette her first orgasm. Maybe her only orgasms. And he was in a crazy mind to do it again.

"Gage," she whispered.

If it'd been a warning, he would have backed out of this. It wasn't one. Far from it. She lifted herself, wrapping her legs around his waist. No more talk that they shouldn't do this. No more anything except her moving into the strokes of his fingers.

Gage wanted to be inside her. And he considered it. But there was going to be enough hell to pay without this becoming full-blown sex against the wall.

Lynette said his name again. And shattered into a thousand little pieces. Gage gathered her in his arms, gave her a moment to catch her breath and then took her to the bed.

Not for sex.

Though his body reminded him of how uncomfortable he was right now.

Still, he had to get some things straight.

"You've gotten over me," he repeated, but it wasn't a

question. The next one wouldn't be, either. "You haven't had sex with another man in ten years. Now, what the devil am I supposed to do with that information?"

She sat up, fixed her clothes and glared at him. Yeah, it was a glare all right. "You're to do nothing with it."

It didn't take long for Gage to figure out why they were having this conversation and not putting this bed to better use.

"This is about your father threatening to kill me," Gage tossed out there.

"It's not a threat. He *will* kill you."

"Not if I kill him first."

She grabbed on to both his arms and got right in his face. But this time, there was no hazy passion glazing her eyes. "And then what? You're arrested and put on death row for killing a state senator?"

Gage didn't even consider that a possibility. "It doesn't have to go down that way. I could force his hand. I doubt it would take much since he already wants me dead."

"And then you've stooped to his level. I won't let you do that for me."

"Then how about I do it for the baby?" he fired back.

"No!" And Lynette didn't whisper it, either. "We do this the right way. We find the evidence to stop him, and we use the justice system to put him in jail for the rest of his life."

"And what if we can't do that?" Gage didn't have to add more because they were both thinking that, with her father around, their baby wouldn't be safe.

"If it comes down to that, then I'll goad him into a fight," Lynette countered. "I'll be the one to kill him."

Gage said a curse word that was so bad that she blinked. "No way will I let you do that. And for the record, it *is* my fight."

He would have said more, cursed more, but the house phone rang, the sound shooting through the room.

"This discussion isn't over," he warned her. Gage snatched up the phone. "What?"

"Having fun?" It was Mason, and he could no doubt tell from Gage's tone that he'd interrupted something.

"Not yet."

"Well, I don't think the fun stuff will start anytime soon."

Gage groaned. "What's wrong?"

"I'm on my way to the guesthouse with the computer so you can watch Grayson's interviews with Nicole, Patrick and Ford." Mason paused. "If the interviews actually happen, that is. You aren't going to believe what they're trying to do to Lynette."

Chapter Nine

Lynette hurried from the shower. Getting the mud and muck off her had felt more like a necessity than a guilty pleasure while Gage and Mason were setting up the equipment so they could watch the interviews. Each second she'd stayed in the steamy hot water, she'd thought of nothing else other than what Mason had told Gage.

You aren't going to believe what they're trying to do to Lynette.

Lynette would believe it because she'd been dealing with them her entire life. She figured all three—Nicole, Patrick and her father—were capable of pretty much anything, and the only thing she could do was shower, ditch the dirty dress she'd been wearing all morning and try to brace herself for the worst.

She found a pair of sweatpants and a denim shirt in the closet and made a mental note to have someone pick her up some clothes and underwear from her house. Her hair was a mess, but clean now, so she combed it with her fingers and made her way back into the living room where she discovered the interview was already in progress.

On the laptop screen, Nicole, Patrick and her father were in an interrogation room at the sheriff's office, all seated at a metal gray table. Grayson was across from them. And behind the three suspects were six lawyers.

"Why are they all in the same room?" she asked Mason. "Shouldn't Grayson be interviewing them separately?"

"He took their initial statements separately, but the three insisted on doing this interview together. Since they haven't been charged with anything, Grayson agreed to accommodate them. Especially since he's trying to defuse something."

"Defuse what?" And Lynette was almost afraid to hear the answer.

Gage got up from the sofa the moment she came in and stepped in front of the screen. He caught on to her arm. "It's not good," he started. "Nicole and your father are trying to have you committed to an asylum."

She was just tired and angry enough to laugh. "Again?" But she couldn't quite choke back those horrible memories of being there. Gage must have seen that in her eyes.

"I'm not going to let that happen," he assured her.

"Neither am I," she let him know with confidence she didn't totally feel. She tipped her head to the laptop screen. "Can they hear us?"

Gage shook his head. "But Mason can text Grayson any question you want him to ask them."

"Good. Then text and ask how they're planning to have me sent back to that place when I'm not insane."

Lynette figured that would prompt a *back to that place?* question from Mason, but he didn't react. Which meant Gage had either filled him in or Nicole and her father had. It was an embarrassing secret, like being a battered spouse, but she figured she'd kept it hidden long enough.

"Your father and Patrick have yet to say a word," Gage explained. "They've let their lawyers do the talking. Nicole, however, has been a regular chatterbox. She says she has documentation to prove you're mentally unstable."

Her stomach tightened. "It's a lie."

"I know," Gage said.

Mason made a sound of agreement. "Our brother's wife Darcy is a hotshot lawyer. We've already got her on this."

Yes, but it could take days, weeks even, and it would embroil Gage's family even deeper in this. "I'll call my father and tell him to back off."

Gage gave her a flat look. "You think that'll help?"

"No. But it'll infuriate him that I'm not begging Nicole and him to play nice."

The corner of Gage's mouth lifted. But then it faded. "Don't call him. I don't want to give him any reason to send another hit man after you."

She shook her head. "We're not even sure he's behind this." Lynette pointed to the screen again where Nicole was babbling on and on about how unstable Lynette was, that Grayson was a fool to believe anything she said.

"Nicole must think I found something on her when I was digging in those old files," Lynette commented.

"Did you?" Mason asked.

"No," she said with plenty of regret. She wished she'd found a mountain of evidence. "So, how do I stop her?"

Gage ran his hand down her arm. "We let Darcy take care of the commitment papers. She said as a minimum she could request an independent medical evaluation for you. That could take days."

"Do we have days?" Lynette asked.

Gage didn't lie—something she appreciated. He just shrugged.

So, that took care of her, temporarily, but it didn't take care of the others. "In the meantime, your family is in danger."

"Don't worry about the family," Mason assured. "We've got all the spouses and the kids covered."

"You're sure?" she pressed. "Because my father and those other two vipers next to him are dangerous. And clever. My father made my mother's murder look like an accident, and I'm sure he can do it again."

Again, Mason didn't look even slightly surprised. "Can we prove it yet?"

"No," Lynette answered. "And trust me, if I could I would trade myself for that confession. That way, at least he'd see the inside of a jail for what he did."

"And you'd be dead," Gage reminded her. "Not going to happen." His hand slid from her arm to her stomach.

That's when Lynette realized that Mason was watching them. His left eyebrow slid up.

"Lynette's pregnant with my baby," Gage admitted. "But no one can know."

Mason made a *hmm* sound. "I knew you two were back together."

"We're not." Again, said in unison.

"It's a long story about the pregnancy," Gage added.

"I know how babies are made," Mason joked, and turned back to the screen.

"Not this baby," Lynette mumbled.

The joking mood vanished. Her father, Patrick and their respective lawyers all stood and exited the interrogation room. So much for Grayson getting them to say anything incriminating.

But Nicole didn't budge. She stayed put, and maybe that meant she was going to give them something. Anything. At this point, Lynette would take a crumb of information if it put them on the right track.

"Lynette's on a vendetta to prove I'm a criminal," Nicole continued.

She huffed, paced, folded her arms over her ample chest. Everything about Nicole screamed that she was a kept woman—the surgical enhancements, the perfect hairstyle, manicure and expensive wardrobe. But Lynette knew Nicole was no dummy. And she wasn't always loyal to Ford. Over the years, the two had fallen out too many times to count. If that happened now, if Nicole and her father ended up on opposite sides, then it could work in their favor.

"I'm going to stop Lynette before she ruins my reputation beyond repair," Nicole continued. She aimed a determined look at Grayson. "If you don't abide by that court order, I'll have your badge."

Then she exited, her lawyers trailing along behind her.

"What court order?" Lynette asked.

Neither Gage nor Mason jumped to answer. Which meant this was bad.

Gage stepped closer to her again. "Grayson has twenty-four hours to escort you to the mental health facility for evaluation."

Oh, God. "And admittance," Lynette supplied.

"Darcy's working on it," Mason reminded her.

Gage continued, "Nicole pulled strings to get that court order. And Darcy's checking into that, too." He lifted her chin, forced eye contact. "There's no way you're going back," he repeated.

Mason turned off the laptop and stuffed it and the equipment into a bag. "I've got to get back to the office and help out Grayson with the investigation. You can handle things here?"

Gage nodded. "When the safe house is ready, I'm moving Lynette."

"Sounds good to me," Mason drawled. He slung the

equipment bag over his shoulder and headed to the door. "They can't serve that court order if they can't find her."

The court order was the least of her worries, but it was a worry.

"Any news on that second hit man?" she asked Gage.

"Not much. I suspect he came with Freddie Denton. Maybe in a backup car. I have someone checking into that."

Yes, no telling how many wheels were turning to try to figure who was behind this and what he or she would do next. After the stunt Nicole had just pulled, the woman was now at the top of her suspect list. Of course, it didn't mean that her father hadn't put Nicole up to doing this.

It made Lynette angry and light-headed just thinking about it, and she headed back to the bedroom in search of some socks. She located a pair in the top dresser drawer.

Gage stayed in the doorway, his shoulder propped against the jamb. Lynette sank down on the foot of the bed. The memory bed. And here she was again in the same room, same bed.

Same man.

And her body was begging her to forget all her worries and seduce Gage. Not that it would require much to get him on the bed with her. They were both operating on a short sexual fuse.

But sex was not going to satisfy them for long.

They had too many things to work out first.

Heck, she wasn't even sure Gage would be around an hour from now much less long enough for them to resolve a decade of hurt and separation.

"I remember the first time I saw you naked," he said. "It was on that very bed, and I thought I'd died and gone to heaven."

Lynette put on the socks. "Gage, that's not helping."

He pushed himself away from the jamb, strolled to her. "It wasn't meant to help." He pulled in a long, weary breath and eased down on his knees in front of her, his body in between her legs.

"Gage," she warned.

"Lynette," he warned right back.

He reached up and pushed her hair from her face. Just that simple touch went through her. Always did.

Gage groaned softly, slid his hands up the outside of her thighs and to her backside. "We have some things to work out before sex," he told her. And he leaned in and buried his face against her breasts.

Just like that her argument started to dissolve.

"But at least all the secrets are out of the way," Gage added. "You know I'm alive. And I know about your father's threat and the baby."

The argument returned in her head. Because all the secrets weren't out of the way.

Well, not one secret anyway.

And it was a huge one.

"What?" Gage asked. He was doing the mind-reading thing again. And would have no doubt pressed her for the truth.

But the phone rang.

Gage gave her a suspicious look, got to his feet and snatched the phone from the nightstand. He didn't say anything, probably because there was no caller ID screen on the old-style phone.

Lynette waited, breath held, and prayed this wasn't bad news. She'd already had enough.

"Hendricks, you have news?" Gage finally said.

Sherman Hendricks, Gage's handler at the CIA.

She watched Gage's expression and body language.

There wasn't much in either to help her figure out what the handler was telling him.

"No," Gage finally said. "Just get that safe house ready." And with that, he hung up.

Lynette got to her feet and faced him.

"It's not good." That's all Gage said for several moments. "The informant who gave us info about the hit man didn't just give the information to us. He gave it and more to the drug lord, Sampson Dalvetti."

Her breath vanished, and she had no choice but to sink back onto the bed. "Dalvetti knows you're alive?"

"It's possible. In fact, Dalvetti might have hired both hit men so he could test the waters. He could have sent them after you. And then leaked it, knowing that if I was alive, it would get back to me."

Oh, mercy. If so, then it'd worked. Dalvetti had maybe figured that Gage would come back from the proverbial grave to save her.

And he had.

But at what cost?

"I'm sorry. So sorry," Gage whispered. He pulled her into his arms.

"You saved my life," she reminded him.

"Yeah. But I'm the one who could have put you in danger in the first place."

She was about to disagree with that, but the phone rang again. He leaned over and punched the button on the base of the phone to put the call on Speaker. However, as a precaution he didn't identify himself.

Good thing, too.

Because it wasn't his handler's voice that greeted them this time.

"Lynette?" the caller said. It was her father.

Gage put his finger to his mouth in a keep-quiet gesture so she wouldn't answer.

"Lynette," Ford continued, "I've called every number at the Ryland ranch, so I figure if you're not listening, you'll get the message." He paused. "I know that Gage is alive."

Her heart went to her knees.

Gage mouthed some profanity. Was this a fishing expedition, or did her father truly know?

"I want to talk to both of you," Ford insisted. "We have things to settle."

Lynette wanted to tell him that talking wasn't going to settle anything between them, but she didn't want her father coming after Gage.

But Gage stood and moved closer to the phone. "Ford, what do you want?" he asked aloud.

Lynette nearly screamed and gave him a look that read, *Have you lost your mind?* Gage ignored her.

"I want to speak to you both, face-to-face," her father informed them. "*Now.* I'm not far away, but your armed ranch hands won't let me onto the property."

"Good," Lynette spoke up. "Because I don't want you here."

"Yes, you do," her father disagreed. "I can call off Nicole, but that'll only happen if you both agree to speak to me."

"Is that so you'll have a better chance at gunning us down?" Gage asked.

"Despite what you think of me, I don't gun down people in broad daylight." He huffed. "I just want to talk to you and my daughter."

"No," Lynette stated as clearly as she could through clenched teeth. "And how exactly did you find out Gage was alive?"

Her father took his time answering, as if he was giving thought to his answer. "If you want to know that, then meet with me. I'll tell you."

Lynette huffed. She didn't want to know it at the risk of her father trying to kill Gage or her.

But Gage turned toward her. Studied her. He mumbled, "I'm sorry." Before she could ask what the devil he meant by that, Gage turned back to the phone. "All right, let's meet," Gage said to her father.

"No!" Lynette insisted.

Gage touched her arm, rubbed gently. Probably a gesture meant to soothe her, but it didn't work. She was far from soothed. She was angry, shocked and frustrated that her father had found out about Gage now. The timing was not good.

"It might help," Gage whispered.

"It might not," she whispered back. "This could be some kind of trick to draw you into a fight."

"That's why you won't be doing this meeting." Gage brushed a kiss on her cheek and turned back to the phone. "Meet me outside the guesthouse. Just me."

"Lynette, too," Ford fired back.

"No deal. Whatever you have to say, you can say it to me."

Chapter Ten

Gage wasn't sure it was the brightest decision to confront Ford, but he was damn tired of the man trying to run roughshod over Lynette. Ford had gotten away with it for, well, all of her life, and maybe the man just needed a good dose of his own bullying tactics.

"I don't want you to do this," Lynette repeated. "It's not safe."

He figured she'd repeat it again before he walked onto the porch to face Ford. "I'll make it safe," Gage promised.

Thankfully, the guesthouse phone had a direct line to the main house and to Mason's ranch office. That's the button that Gage pushed.

"Ford Herrington's at the end of the road," Mason informed him the second he answered.

"Yeah. I'm meeting him to settle some things."

Mason paused. "Lynette couldn't talk you out of it?" He didn't wait for an answer. "You always were the hardheaded one."

Gage couldn't argue with that. "How many ranch hands are with Ford right now?"

"Two. I had them stand guard at the top of the road so we wouldn't get any unexpected visitors. Both are armed, and I trust them."

Good. If Mason trusted them, then so did Gage. "Call

them for me and have them escort Ford to the guesthouse. I'll meet them out front."

Mason paused again, and Gage waited for his brother to try to talk him out of this confrontation, but then Mason just cursed and hung up. One down, another to go. He looked at Lynette, who was fuming, and knew this was another argument he had to win.

"Why don't you get something to eat while I talk to your father?" Gage knew the lame suggestion would fall on her deaf ears so he played dirty. He glanced down at her stomach. "Think of the baby. It's not good for you to go this long without eating."

Her eyes narrowed, and she called him a bad name that questioned his intelligence and his paternity. But she turned and headed for the kitchen.

"I'm watching from the window," she informed him.

Good grief. He wasn't the only hardheaded person in the room. "Stay back. Away from the glass."

That got her whirling around to face him again. No more narrowed eyes, but there was worry in them now. Gage went to her, slid his arm around her. Kissed her.

Then, kissed her again.

"That won't work," she snarled against his mouth.

"Yeah. It will. Because you're going to think of the baby again and play it safe."

"That's not fair."

"I know. But I can't carry this baby," he reminded her. "Only you can do that. And that means I do the caveman stuff and you grow us a healthy child."

Gage didn't miss how easily the *us* had flowed off his tongue. There was a lot for them to work out before there was an *us,* and it started with this meeting with Ford.

He drew his Glock from his holster, took a deep breath and stepped onto the porch. Gage also checked to make sure Lynette wasn't right by the window. And that she was eating.

A winner on both counts.

She was munching on an apple as if she were in a race to finish it, and while she was close to the front door and window, she was staying back.

It didn't take long—less than a minute—for the truck to come to a stop in front of the guesthouse. An armed ranch hand was on either side of Ford, and they all got out. The ranch hands stopped at the white picket fence gate. Not Ford. He walked toward Gage.

"That's close enough," Gage told the man when he made it to the bottom step. It was still drizzling and Ford didn't have an umbrella, but Gage hoped the discomfort of the weather would speed things up. He didn't want Ford on the grounds any longer than necessary.

"How did you find out I was alive?" Gage tossed out there for starters.

Ford lifted his shoulder. "I have my sources."

"And those would be?" Gage pressed.

"Confidential."

Gage wished he could wipe that smugness off Ford's weaselly face, but that would only make this ordeal last longer. Best to hear what he had to say and then get him far away from the ranch.

"I haven't told anyone you're alive," Ford insisted.

Gage didn't believe him, but he had more important things to discuss. "Call off Nicole."

He lifted his shoulder again. "I'll try."

"On the phone you said you could do it. That's the only reason I'm out here."

"I said I would if you both agreed to talk to me." Ford made a show of looking at Gage. "You're not *both*."

Gage heard the movement behind him and cursed a

blue streak. That's because Lynette opened the blasted door and came out onto the porch with him. He shot her a warning glance, which did no good whatsoever.

"Now, you have both," Lynette snarled. "Call off your lover."

Her father seemed more than pleased that he'd gotten his way.

"I'll put pressure on Nicole," Ford told them. "I know some of her secrets." He paused a heartbeat. "Yours, too." And he was looking at Lynette when he said it.

Hell. Did Ford know about the baby?

It wasn't something Lynette could keep secret for long because she would soon start showing, but Gage hadn't wanted Ford to put two and two together and come up with the conclusion of the baby being Gage's. That would only start another war between Ford and him. Gage needed some security measures in place so that Lynette wouldn't be anywhere near her father when he learned she was pregnant.

"Yes, secrets," Lynette repeated. She tried to step around him, but Gage blocked her. He couldn't hog-tie her and put her back inside the house, but by God, as a minimum he could shield her body with his. "You mean like the secret you told me about my mother?"

A muscle flickered in Ford's jaw, but that was his only response. "That was a long time ago."

"Yes, there's no statute of limitations on murder," she fired back.

Gage didn't want to take his eyes off Ford, but he turned around and gave Lynette another warning glance. This was turning ugly fast.

"There's also a law against bribing a public official," Ford said, pulling Gage's attention back to him.

Gage braced himself for Lynette to ask what the heck that meant, but she didn't say anything.

Oh, man.

"You didn't think I'd find out?" Ford snapped, his attention still nailed to Lynette. "I *always* find out everything you do."

"What are you talking about?" Gage just came out and asked.

Ford got that smug look again. "She didn't tell you?" He clucked his tongue. "Lynette's one for secrets. All that digging into my personal files prompted me to do some more digging, too. She bought a condo in Dallas, and she used an assumed name. Did she tell you that?"

No. But Gage guessed that's where she'd planned to go when she could no longer hide the pregnancy. It was a smart move, but it hurt for Gage to think she'd had to do these smart moves on her own. And because they'd been necessary.

"What does that have to do with bribing an official?" Gage pressed.

"I need to talk to you," Lynette whispered to him.

That put a big knot in his belly.

"See, it's different when it's your secrets being blabbed, isn't it?" Ford questioned. "I figured you'd done the right thing about the annulment, especially after I'd made it so clear what the consequences would be if you didn't. Imagine my surprise when last month I discovered you'd bribed an official. A judge, no less."

Gage shook his head. "What the hell is this about?"

Ford smiled. "What my daughter needs to tell you is that you two are still married."

LYNETTE FELT THE BLOOD drain from her head, and she was sorry she'd wolfed down that apple, because she was suddenly queasy, too. She'd intended to tell Gage about the annulment. Or rather the lack of one.

But she darn sure hadn't wanted to tell him like this.

She looked at Gage, lowered her voice, so she could tell him something meant only for his ears. "I bribed a judge in Kerrville to fake the annulment."

Gage blinked. Looked at Ford then her. "We're still married?"

Lynette nodded. "Don't read too much into it," she added.

He stared at her. The same stare he'd given her when she'd told him he was the only lover she'd ever had. There was a reason for that.

She'd always considered herself a married woman.

That, and she hadn't wanted another man. Just Gage. And her father was going to do everything in his power to make sure she didn't get him.

Not then, not now.

"Any reason you didn't tell me this?" Gage asked her.

She tipped her head to her father. "The reason is standing out there in the rain."

"I told her I'd kill you if she didn't get the annulment," Ford volunteered. "Never wanted her to drop in bed with the likes of you. Her tramp of a mother already did that with your kin."

Some venom went through Gage's eyes, and he turned that venom on her father. "It takes a special kind of man to use a threat like that on a nineteen-year-old girl. But guess what? Lynette and I aren't kids anymore, and I've been trained to take out scum like you."

"Is that a threat?" Ford snapped.

"You bet it is." Gage took one step forward, and in the same motion, he pushed her behind him. "If you come near Lynette, if you utter another threat to her—veiled or otherwise—you're going down."

Ford chuckled. "You'd kill me in cold blood, *Agent* Ryland?"

"No." Gage's voice got eerily calm. "I'd wait until you pulled your gun first. But trust me, I'm faster. I can get a bullet in your brain so quick that before you blink, you'll already be in hell."

Oh, mercy.

Lynette had to do something to defuse this. It was already past taking a dangerous turn.

"I'm about to faint," Lynette whispered to him. And she prayed she sounded convincing enough. "Please. I don't want to fall. It might hurt the baby."

That got Gage moving. "Get *him* out of here," Gage told the ranch hands.

Gage kept his eyes on her father and his right hand on his gun, but he looped his left arm around her and got her inside. He kicked the door shut, lifted her into arms and took her to the sofa.

"Should I call the doctor?" Gage asked, looking down at her. No more venom in his voice. Just worry.

Well, for a couple of seconds.

"You're not about to faint," he accused. Gage cursed. "That's playing dirty, Lynette."

She came off the sofa. "I didn't want you in a gunfight with my father. This is what I've been trying to prevent for over a decade."

His anger and frustration returned with a vengeance. Gage kicked a wood magazine holder next to the sofa and hurried to the door. He looked out. Cursed some more. And locked it as if he'd declared war on it. He reholstered his gun and started to pace like a caged tiger.

"I'm not sorry for what I did," she let him know.

Still pacing, he aimed his index finger at her. He also tried to speak, but the anger didn't let the words come. Not that she wanted to hear what he had to say right now. Lynette had warned him that talking to her father would be bad, and Gage hadn't listened.

"I'm not sorry about the nonannulment, either," she added. Best to clear the air about that, as well, since Gage was going to stew for a while.

The burst of temper drained her, and Lynette dropped back down onto the sofa. Gage studied her a moment, and his pacing took him back to the door where he armed the security system. He then paced to the kitchen and came back with a Lone Star beer and a pint-size carton of milk.

"Drink," he ordered.

"Well, since you asked so nicely…" Lynette took the milk.

"Don't," he warned her. "If you'd told me we were still married—"

"My father would have picked a fight with you sooner," she interrupted. "Just remember, there's a reason I tried to make him think I'd gone through with the annulment."

His thumb whacked against his chest. "Yeah. To save me. Lynette, I didn't need saving. Not at that price!"

"The price was worth it to me."

He gulped down a good portion of the beer, and it was obvious he was still wrestling with the bombshell that her father had just delivered. "How much did it cost you to bribe the official?"

She took a moment, drank some milk, dodged his gaze. "Ten thousand," she mumbled.

His mouth dropped open. And she knew why. Her father was rich, but he'd never shared that wealth with her. She'd worked for every penny that she had in the bank.

Which wasn't much, considering she had a mortgage for the condo in Dallas and her house in Silver Creek.

"Where'd you get that kind of money?" Gage demanded.

She decided it was a good time to avoid his gaze some more. "I sold my mother's jewelry."

The profanity was there, in his eyes, but he didn't voice it. Instead, he sank down onto the coffee table across from her. "Not her gold heart necklace?"

Lynette nodded. "All of it."

"What about your wedding ring?" he asked.

"I kept that." She didn't manage to say that above a whisper, but Gage no doubt heard it loud and clear.

Lynette undid the top button on her shirt so she could reach her bra. She pulled the ring from the tiny pocket she'd sewn into the right cups of all her bras and held it up for him to see.

"My father has a bad habit of searching my place when I'm not there," she explained. "I figured it was best if I kept it on me as much as possible. Less chance of him finding it." She slipped the ring back into her bra. Rebuttoned her shirt.

Now he cursed, but there was no anger in it. "If you tell me you're over me, I'll…"

"Take me where I stand?" she finished, hoping the levity would help.

He shot her a scowl. "I'll make you take a nap." Gage groaned. "If you'd just told me…" He didn't finish that, either. Didn't need to.

"It probably seems selfish and a little crazy on my part, but I wanted to hang on to the marriage as long as I could because it was my way of hanging on to you. I knew that you'd get on with your life. That you'd find someone else and when you did, I'd planned to get a quick annulment so you wouldn't be committing bigamy." She paused. "But you didn't find anyone else. Not that I know of anyway."

Another scowl. "No." He drained more of the beer. "And I didn't have to sell something I loved or keep a secret that burned into my soul."

"Yes, you did," she reminded him. "You left your family. Faked your death to save me and your brothers. If we're comparing our martyr badges, I think they're about the same size."

He looked at her. "So, where does that leave us?"

Lynette drank her milk. "Our martyrdom failed. Even after all these years, we're right back where we started. Married and in danger."

"Yeah." And that's all he said for a long time.

Except this time around, the danger was even worse. Because it wasn't just Gage and her. Their baby was now involved in this.

Gage set his beer aside, stood, and without warning, he scooped her up. "You're taking that nap," he growled. *"Alone,"* he added, heading for the bedroom. "I have some things to work out."

"You're not leaving?" she asked.

"No." A moment later, he repeated it along with a heavy sigh and deposited her onto the bed. "I don't want you here by yourself."

His gaze dropped from her face, to her body.

All of her body.

Lynette could have seduced him to make him stay in the room with her. She could keep an eye on him that way and make sure that he didn't go after her father.

Of course, seducing Gage had other benefits, too.

Her body was always burning for him. Plus, she was already on the bed with him just inches away, and she knew his weak spots. Some neck kisses would get this seduction started the right way.

But she had some things to work out, as well.

Like how she was going to neutralize her father. She'd been trying to work it out for ten years now, and it was past time she came up with a permanent solution.

But what?

Her investigation had failed to turn up anything, but maybe that just meant she had to dig deeper or in a different place. Maybe she could get someone at the asylum in Mexico to spill what her father had done to her. It wasn't a good angle, but it might be the only one they had.

"I'll keep digging," she promised him.

He shook his head. "After you rest."

Gage leaned down, and for a moment she thought he had changed his mind about joining her. But his mouth didn't go in the direction of hers. Instead, he dropped a kiss on her stomach.

On the baby.

The moment was so perfect, so sweet, that it brought tears to her eyes.

"Get some sleep." He threw the covers over her and walked out.

Lynette watched him stride away in those jeans that hugged his best asset. Well, one of them anyway. His heart was at the top of that asset list.

A tear spilled down her cheek.

Loving Gage seemed to be something she couldn't stop. Even though loving him was the fastest way to get him killed.

Lynette pulled the covers to her chin and knew that the only way to save him was to say goodbye.

Again.

Chapter Eleven

Gage's eyes flew open. He groaned and got up from the sofa where he'd fallen asleep. His thirty-minute catnap had turned into four hours. His body had needed rest, but he should have been thinking and planning instead of dozing off.

Planning how to bring Ford Herrington down.

He stumbled toward the bedroom, and nearly had a heart attack when he didn't see Lynette where he'd left her.

"I'm in the kitchen," she called out to him.

He turned to hurry to her, bashed his knee against the doorjamb and had to go into the kitchen limping. But the hurrying up wasn't necessary. Lynette was seated at the country-style kitchen table eating—Gage looked at her plate—pancakes smeared with crunchy peanut butter.

"You okay?" she asked, glancing at the knee that he was rubbing.

Gage nodded. "You?"

She nodded, too. Lynette slid some of the pancakes onto another plate and passed them his way.

His stomach growled, and Gage realized the only thing he'd had to eat or drink in the past twenty-four hours was a beer. Hardly food for thoughts and planning. He grabbed a fork from the drawer and dug in. It wasn't steak and eggs, his favorite, but it was good.

"Thanks," he mumbled.

Lynette poured him a glass of milk, set it next to his plate and then sank down in the chair across from him. Uh-oh. That look in her baby blues told him this wasn't going to be a conversationless meal.

And they *should* talk, he reminded himself.

But for a moment he let himself take all of this in. Lynette and he doing something as ordinary as sharing a meal. Of course, ordinary and Lynette didn't fit. An oxymoron. She was anything but.

"What are you looking at?" she asked. And made him smile when she ran her hand over her shoulder-length blond hair to smooth it down.

"You," he admitted. "You're prettier now than when you were seventeen. Wouldn't have thought that was possible, because you caught a lot of eyes even then."

She blushed. Made him smile again. "Look at yourself in the mirror, Gage Ryland. You're the hot guy every girl in high school wanted in their dreams. And in their beds. I was just lucky enough to get you in mine."

The last part had her looking uncomfortable and glancing away. "Sorry," she mumbled.

He shrugged. "You don't have to say the words aloud to make me think of being in bed with you." And he waited to see where that would take him.

Apparently, not far.

When her gaze returned to his, she looked serious again. "When I was at the asylum in Mexico, there was a nurse, Rosa Mendez, who was nice to me. She seemed to believe me when I told her that I'd been sent there against my will and that I wasn't crazy. I want to see if I can find her. Maybe she'll have some proof that my father had me committed there illegally."

Gage gave that some thought, but he didn't have to think long or hard to see where this could go.

"I doubt Ford left that kind of loose end behind." And if he did, he would just neutralize her before she could give them anything they could use. However, he didn't say that to Lynette. "But I'll check into it."

And he would make sure this Rosa Mendez had some protection. Of course, protection hadn't worked so far.

"It could be a good lead," Gage assured her with confidence he didn't feel.

She nodded, stared at him. "If you don't swear to me that you'll stay away from my father, then I'm leaving when I finish these pancakes. I'll call Mason to come and get me, and I'm out that door."

Oh, man. That was an ultimatum he hadn't seen coming. "It's not safe for you to go."

"And it's not safe for you if I stay."

Gage had another bite of the pancake that he no longer wanted. "No deal. Your father won't quit just because I back off."

"Maybe not. But he might if I tell him I'm going to the press, that I'll do an interview with every tabloid in Texas, and I'll tell them how he confessed to killing my mother."

Gage started shaking his head. She ignored him.

"I'll tell my father that I'll convince the new assistant district attorney, who happens to be your sister-in-law, to take the case to a grand jury. I've never had anyone in the D.A.'s office on my side, but I do now with Darcy." She paused. "I'll also tell him that the way to stop me is to leave you the hell alone."

Gage groaned, stood and went to her. He pulled her

to her feet and then into his arms. "What the devil am I going to do with you?"

One thing he did know. Lynette was not going to fight his battles for him.

She didn't exactly melt against him. "You're going to agree to leave for a while until things settle down."

He blinked, pulled back so he could see her stubborn face. "I'm not going anywhere."

"It's not a choice. If you want to drop kisses on my baby belly and make me cry." Her voice quivered a little, and she cleared her throat. "If you want a chance for us to try to work things out, then you have to leave."

He stared at her. "Let me get this straight. Both scenarios involve leaving. You in the first one. Me, in the second. That's going to be hard to do because I don't intend to let you out of my sight until the danger has passed. Remember the hit men who tried to kill you?"

"I remember." She swallowed hard.

Gage hated that he shoved those nightmares right back at her, but he wasn't backing down. "No one will do more to protect you and this baby than I will," he promised her.

She opened her mouth to argue, but thankfully the phone mounted to the wall rang. Without taking his attention from her, he reached over and pushed the speaker button to answer the call.

"Gage," the caller said.

Not Ford or one of his brothers. But his handler, Sherman Hendricks.

Gage didn't miss the tone in Sherman's greeting, and he reached to take the call off Speaker. But Lynette stopped him. She gave him a look, reminding him that she had the right to know. And she did.

"This is about Dalvetti?" Gage asked his handler.

"Yes." Sherman's pause was long enough to make Gage

more than uncomfortable. "We've confirmed that Dalvetti knows you're alive."

Gage automatically went to the window, lifted the blinds and looked out. "How'd you confirm it?"

"Dalvetti left a message with the informant who told us about the hit man who was after Ms. Herrington. The now-dead informant. Dalvetti carved the message on the guy's chest and stomach. It said, *This time Gage Ryland dies for real.*"

Gage checked to make sure Lynette was okay. She wasn't. She sank back onto the chair. He cursed himself for not doing it sooner, but he grabbed the phone from the receiver and took the call off Speaker. Of course, the damage had already been done.

"The safe house is nearly ready," Sherman continued. "We had to take even more precautions than we normally take."

And those extra precautions might not be nearly enough. "Finish the preparations for it and send two agent decoys there. Because Dalvetti might have an informant in the CIA."

Sherman didn't jump to say that wasn't possible. It was. And both of them knew it. Dalvetti could already know the location of the safe house. Heck, he could know that Lynette was with him.

"What are you going to do?" Sherman asked.

Gage looked out the window again. "I'd rather not say. I trust you, Sherman, but the less you know, the better." Gage didn't wait for him to agree. "How long do I have before Dalvetti comes here?"

"A day, maybe less."

Well, it wasn't good news, but it was better than the drug lord being on the front porch.

"I'll be in touch," Gage promised Sherman.

By the time he hung up, Lynette was on her feet again and coming toward him. "Gage" was all she managed to say.

The fear on her face was enough to make him sick, and so that he wouldn't make that fear worse, Gage clamped down his own feelings.

"The safe house wouldn't be a good idea," he explained. "But I can do things to make you safe."

Gage sat and pulled her onto his lap. It was wrong to leach comfort from her this way, but by God, he needed to have her in his arms right now. That didn't stop him from taking the phone again and calling Mason.

"I'll make this quick," Gage said the second Mason answered. "The drug lord is coming to Silver Creek, and it won't take him long to find the ranch. You need to get everyone out of here."

If Mason had a reaction to that, he didn't voice it. "How much time do we have?"

"Do it as fast as possible. You have a place to go?"

"Dade's wife has a place in San Antonio. We had to use it a couple of months ago when there was trouble at the ranch." Mason paused. "But we have a little problem this time around. Eve just went into labor."

Eve, Grayson's wife. Gage loved her like the sister he'd never had, but it was not a good time for her to be giving birth.

"Grayson's on the way to the hospital with her," Mason added.

Of course he was, but Grayson would be tied up with the delivery and he wouldn't be thinking about security.

"Kade's heading to the hospital to be with them, too," Mason went on.

Good. His little brother Kade was an FBI agent and

could protect them. That would leave Dade and Nate to get the wives and children to San Antonio.

"I'm staying with you?" Mason asked as if he'd already grasped the plan that Gage hadn't even come up with yet.

"I'd like family backup," Gage admitted.

"Then you got it." And Mason didn't hesitate.

Until that moment Gage hadn't realized how much he'd missed his family. And how lucky he was to be a Ryland.

"What about Lynette?" Mason asked.

"I'm handling that now."

Gage glanced at Lynette to see how much he had to handle with her. But she wasn't panicking. If anything, now that the initial shock had worn off, she looked resolved to the danger.

That riled him even more.

Danger should have never entered her life, and now she had so much that heaven knows what the stress was doing to her and the baby.

Gage had to do something.

But what he couldn't do was go off half-cocked. His instincts were to cram Lynette into the nearest vehicle and drive out of there fast. But there had to be some things in place first. And he didn't want to take Lynette to the house in San Antonio with the others because the danger might follow them there.

"Call me when you've worked things out with Lynette," Mason insisted, and he ended the call.

"Good news," he started. "Eve's having her baby."

Lynette managed a smile of sorts. Brief and barely. But there. She slid her hand over her stomach and was hopefully thinking one day she'd be there, safe in the hospital. Giving birth.

That seemed like an eternity from now.

"There could be a bright side in all of this," he said to

her. "Maybe your father, Nicole or Patrick didn't try to have you killed after all."

"Maybe," she repeated, clearly in deep thought. Lynette wasn't a coward, but right now she had to be worried about the safety of the baby she was carrying.

Gage was worried, too.

Because even if Ford wasn't guilty of attempted murder, he'd still murdered. Sooner or later, Gage was going to have settle that score.

He pulled her closer, careful not to touch any part of her that would distract them. Lynette and he had a problem with touching. It always turning to kissing and kissing led to sex. She didn't need that right now. And he vetoed his body's suggestion that it would help her get her mind off things.

Nothing was going to do that.

"How will Dalvetti come after us?" she asked, slicing right to the point.

"Not us. *Me*. You'll be at the main house with Mason and as many armed ranch hands as he has guarding you."

She stared at him. "You're going after Dalvetti?"

Gage figured a lie would just put more fire in her eyes. "I have to. If I don't, he'll try to use you and my family to get revenge against me."

A thin breath left her mouth. "You could stay at the house with Mason and me."

He shook his head. "I have to end this, Lynette."

"But it's dangerous."

"It's my job. It's what I do, and believe it or not, I'm really good at it." He shrugged. "Well, most days. I screwed up with the informant."

"No. You didn't. Because Denton would have killed me and the baby if you hadn't stopped him."

Gage had a hard time even imagining that, and he

didn't care how many people he had to take down to keep her safe.

"I know I wasn't in on the planning stage of this baby," he said, "but so you know, I want it."

He expected that to soothe her because the words sure as heck soothed him and put things crystal clear in his mind. But she grabbed on to his arm—hard.

"That sounds like a goodbye, and it'd better not be."

He shook his head. "No goodbye. I'm coming back, and we'll work out the rest. Got that?"

Gage wanted to hear her answer, but the blasted phone rang again. Because it could be his handler with more information, he answered it right away.

"It's me," Mason greeted. "The others just drove out of here using the back way to get to the highway. Don't worry. We have that trail closed off for any other traffic. But they had to use it this time because there's a visitor at the end of the road where the two guards are. It's Patrick Harkin."

Not now. "What the heck does he want?" Gage barked.

"To talk to Lynette and you. I gotta say, you two are popular with the scumbag crowd. Patrick says he wants to explain how Ford found out you were alive."

Definitely not now. "Tell him to call me tomorrow." Gage doubted he would be there then.

"I tried that. Tried telling him I'd arrest him for trespassing, but he claims it's important. Says it has to do with the drug lord."

"Dalvetti?"

"The very one," Mason verified. "I'm on my way to the guesthouse now so I can bring the computer to monitor the security cameras. If you want, I can have one of the ranch hands escort Patrick to the front yard."

No, it wasn't what Gage wanted. He didn't want Patrick within a mile of Lynette. But Gage also needed some answers. *Any* answers that would stop an attack, and Patrick might be able to provide those.

"I'll meet you in the yard in a couple of minutes," Gage told him. He hung up and immediately turned to Lynette. "And this time, you *will* stay inside. You won't argue about it, either," he added when she opened her mouth.

"I wasn't going to argue. I was going to tell you to be careful. And to give me a gun for backup. I've been doing target practice in the woods behind my house, and I'm a good shot."

Gage didn't doubt it, but he knew he didn't want Lynette having to shoot a gun at anyone. Still, he opened the cabinet above the fridge and saw that it was still there. His grandfather's old Colt .45. He checked to see if it was loaded. It was. And he put it in her waiting hand.

"Stay inside," Gage repeated. "Away from the windows." He pressed a kiss on her cheek. And decided that was a sucky way for him to go out that door.

So he kissed her the right way.

He snapped her to him and put his mouth to hers. Yeah. The right way. His lips, moving over hers. He waited for the slight moan that he knew she'd make.

She made it.

And he kept the kiss long, slow and deep. Gage pulled away from her and was pleased they were both breathing hard. If he was going to muddy the waters with Lynette, he might as well do a thorough job of it.

Or so he kept telling himself.

He was doing that so he could justify the way he was complicating the heck out of things. He wasn't free to think about a relationship with her. Not yet. And even after this situation with Dalvetti was over, they still had obstacles to face.

Gage drew his gun and stepped outside. The rain had stopped, finally, and it was late afternoon, still plenty of light. For now. But it wouldn't be long before the sun set. It also would be a god-awful long night without some kind of information that Gage was hoping he'd get from the weasel of a visitor.

He glanced toward the ranch house and saw Mason driving up in the rust-scarred pickup truck that had seen better days. It was his usual mode of transportation, and he wouldn't budge on getting anything new. In the other direction, Gage spotted one of the ranch hands escorting Patrick. Not in a vehicle.

But walking.

The other ranch hand was still at the end of the road next to the sleek black luxury car. Patrick's, no doubt.

"His car died," the ranch hand called out. "He couldn't get it to start."

"Then he'll be walking back into town," Mason said, stepping from his truck. He had a stuffed-full equipment bag. "Because I'm not tying up any of my men for the likes of him."

Gage couldn't agree more. Now, he just needed to hurry this along so he could make sure the guesthouse was as safe as it could be.

"I need to put this inside," Mason let him know, and he carried in the equipment bag. A few seconds later, he came back out. "I told Lynette to boot up the laptop so we can keep an eye on all the security cameras."

Good idea. As long as she stayed put.

"Start talking," Gage said while Patrick was still walking toward the guesthouse.

"You have a big problem," Patrick answered.

"If you're here to state the obvious, then you can turn around and leave," Gage answered back.

When Patrick reached the fence, he started to open the gate, but Mason stopped him. "You can state more than the obvious from right where you are."

Patrick's mouth tightened, and he eyed them both as if they were scum. Which made Gage wonder—if he hated them so much, then why was he here? Gage doubted the man had good intentions, but sometimes bad intentions worked just as well. Especially if Patrick could give them anything that would put an end to Dalvetti and his threats. It was telling that Patrick even knew about the drug lord. It meant he had at least something.

"Ford isn't going to let this go," Patrick went on.

Again, it was the obvious, and Gage's eye roll let him know that. "The subject you wanted to discuss was Dalvetti." But Gage paused. "Unless Ford has some connection there. If so, spill it and don't waste any more of my time.

Patrick swallowed hard. "I want a deal. Immunity from prosecution."

A deal? It wasn't totally unexpected, but it didn't have anything to do with Dalvetti. Or it damn well shouldn't.

"What have you done that would warrant prosecution?" Gage asked when Patrick didn't add more.

Patrick glanced around. The look of a man on edge. "Ford has some things on me. Things he said he'd leak if I don't cooperate and do as he says." He paused again. "He wants me to kidnap Lynette so he can get her the psychiatric help she needs."

Gage tried very hard not to curse. But he failed. "Lynette's not crazy. Ford is. And what kind of dirt does he have on you?"

More glancing around. "Business deals. Buried away a long time ago. You'd never find them, but Ford apparently kept copies of things."

"I'll bet he did." Gage glanced around, too. The weasel was making him nervous, and he still hadn't spilled anything about Dalvetti. "So, why come to me? Why not just go on being Ford's lackey?"

He dipped down his head a little. "Because I don't want to be part of what Ford's trying to do to Lynette."

"You're just a regular do-gooder, aren't you?" Mason snarled.

Patrick's next round of glances included his car. It was just a glance, but Gage had dealt with scum long enough to know something was wrong.

Gage lifted his gun. "You've got five seconds to tell me why you're really here, and your explanation better include the name Dalvetti."

Patrick shook his head.

Gage took aim at him.

Patrick threw his hands up in the air. "Ford made a deal with Dalvetti." He said the words so quickly that it took Gage a moment to understand what he'd blurted out.

"I'm sorry," Patrick said. "I didn't have a choice."

Hell.

"What did you do?" Gage demanded.

Patrick only shook his head again.

Gage looked at him. At the stalled vehicle. And at the ranch hand near the car.

"Get down!" Gage shouted to the hand.

The ranch hand immediately dived to the side, but it was already too late.

The car exploded in a fireball.

Patrick dropped to the ground, his hands sheltering his head.

"What did you do?" Gage yelled to Patrick.

Patrick kept his head down, but Gage heard him loud and clear. "Dalvetti is *here*."

Chapter Twelve

The sound of the explosion sent Lynette racing to the window.

Oh, God.

Patrick's car had blown to smithereens. Just like the plane at the airport.

She watched Patrick drop to the ground, saw him say something that had Gage throwing open the door and running inside toward her.

"Get down," he told her.

Mason was right behind him, his phone sandwiched between his shoulder and his ear, and he was barking out instructions to someone on the other end of the line.

"What's going on?" she asked Gage.

He caught on to her arm and headed for the bathroom. Without a word, he pulled back the plastic curtain of the tub-shower combo, and he put her inside.

Gage looked her straight in the eyes. "According to Patrick, Dalvetti and your father are in on this together. And Dalvetti is here on the grounds."

Everything inside her went still. The calm before the storm, no doubt. But it was going to take a few seconds for it to sink in that a cold-blooded killer was at the ranch and that her father was perhaps responsible for his being here.

Not perhaps, she amended.

Almost certainly.

This is exactly the kind of destructive stunt he would pull, and he would have no trouble sending Patrick to do his dirty work.

"Where is Dalvetti?" she managed to ask.

Gage shook his head. "I don't know, but I'll find out."

And that meant he would go out there looking for this monster.

Lynette caught on to his arm, to beg him to stay inside, but Mason called out to them. "The ranch hand near the explosion is okay. He hasn't seen anyone other than Patrick."

But then, Mason cursed.

Her breath froze. And she waited to hear the bad news that had caused the profanity. There was no mistaking from Mason's tone that it would be *bad.*

Gage hurried out of the room, and Lynette moved in the tub so she could see them in the doorway of the bedroom. Mason was carrying the laptop and showed the screen to Gage.

"Someone's blocked all the feed from the security cameras," she heard Gage say. "We can't see a thing."

No. That couldn't happen. They needed those cameras to pinpoint Dalvetti's location. Especially with the sun setting. There were plenty of places for him to hide and then sneak up on the guesthouse.

"I'll keep an eye on Patrick and the front of the guesthouse," Mason let him know, and he handed Gage the laptop and headed back out.

"How bad is this?" she asked.

Gage came back into the bathroom and put the laptop on the side of the tub. "If the feed comes back on, let me know. If Dalvetti or someone else is using a jammer, he might not be able to keep an interference signal for long."

Lynette looked at the screen. No images. Just white static.

Gage disappeared into the living room where she could hear him rummaging around, and he came back with his grandfather's Colt, extra ammunition and a walkie-talkie.

"Mason brought the walkie-talkie in the equipment bag," he explained. His gaze finally came to hers and held. "If Dalvetti gets past Mason and me, shoot him."

She wanted to ask what were the odds of him making it into the house, but Lynette really didn't want to know. Because there was only one way Dalvetti would manage to make it inside, and that's if Gage and Mason were dead.

That couldn't happen.

Somehow they all had to make it out of this.

"I'll be careful," Gage promised her before she even demanded that he say it.

He popped a kiss on her mouth and left again. This time, she heard him leave by the front door.

Lynette hugged her knees to her chest, but she kept the Colt in her hand. Ready. Well, hopefully. She'd done lots of target practice, but she doubted a man like Dalvetti would just stand there while she took aim and shot him.

And he might not be alone.

He'd probably brought some hired guns and a lot of weapons with him. Worse, he might even have had help from her father planning this attack.

She listened, trying to pick through the sounds outside. She heard voices, and there was movement around the exterior of the guesthouse, but it was impossible to tell what was going on.

There was a slight clicking sound, and Lynette's attention flew to the laptop screen. It was no longer white static. The images came on, one by one, until there were six of them on the screen. Each shot showed a different camera angle of the ranch.

Still holding on to the gun, she pulled the laptop closer, her gaze rifling over each one.

Finally, she saw Gage.

Thank God.

It wasn't the best camera view, but he was in the yard in front of the guesthouse. A rifle was in one hand and his Glock was in his shoulder holster. He was hunched down as if prepared for an attack. However, the white picket fence wouldn't give him much protection if bullets started flying. Patrick was in the shallow ditch just in front of that fence, looking ready to run off in a panic.

Lynette didn't care a flip about his fear, because Patrick had had a part in setting all of this up. In fact, he'd no doubt used this meeting to distract them in some way so that Dalvetti could jam those cameras and come onto the ranch.

Her attention darted to all the monitors. She saw Mason on one of the other cameras. He was somewhere behind the guesthouse and was directing ranch hands. The men, at least a half dozen of them, were all armed and scattering out. She prayed it would be enough.

The other cameras were positioned in the back pasture, the road and the front and rear of the main house. Things looked normal. Definitely no sign of Dalvetti, her father or any other gunmen. But then, her father wouldn't do this in person. No. He wouldn't put himself in danger, only others. Including Gage and her baby.

That sent a shot of raw anger through her.

When this was over, she had to figure out how to stop this from happening again and again.

Lynette kept her attention pinned to the laptop. And because she was watching so closely, she saw the movement. Not near the guesthouse but near the entrance to the ranch where Patrick's car was still blazing.

Two men came bolting from across the road.

They were dressed in dark green camouflage clothes and were armed with assault rifles. Behind them trailed another man, also armed with a rifle and other guns holstered in an equipment belt.

The last man was no doubt Dalvetti.

Lynette had never seen a picture of him, nor had she even heard a description, but she was certain that's who it was. He moved like a man in charge. Like a man on a mission of murder. And he and those men were using the smoke from Patrick's vehicle for cover.

Lynette jabbed the button on the walkie-talkie, and she both saw and heard Gage answer.

"The cameras are working. Three men just crossed the road near Patrick's car," she relayed with her voice shaking.

"Keep watching and stay put," Gage warned her again.

She saw him use the walkie-talkie to speak to someone else. Mason, she realized. Because Mason said something into his own walkie-talkie and started toward the road.

When she started to get dizzy, Lynette realized she was holding her breath. She wouldn't be any good to Gage and the others if she fainted, so she reminded herself to breathe.

The three guys in camo made it to the burning car but then climbed over the white fence that lined each side of the road. The opposite side of the guesthouse, but still with those rifles, they were possibly already in firing range.

Lynette pressed the button on the walkie-talkie. "The three men are in the east pasture now. They're using the fence and the smoke from the explosion to hide."

Gage didn't respond right away, but she saw him turn in that direction. "I see them." He clicked off the walkie-talkie.

Just as the shot blasted through the air.

Gage dived for cover on the side of the porch steps. Some of the ranch hands hit the ground. Mason ducked behind a tree. Patrick crawled closer to the fence but stayed in the meager cover of the ditch.

Another shot.

She couldn't see which of the three men were shooting, but she did see Gage lift the rifle. He also levered himself up and out of the meager cover of the steps.

Gage fired.

So did Mason.

Lynette watched their bullets tear into the wooden fence. The shots, however, didn't stop the trio.

More bullets came, and one slammed into the guesthouse. But not just into the guesthouse—in the bedroom just yards from where she was. She pulled the computer onto her lap and sank down lower into the tub. She couldn't risk one of those shots hitting her because it would endanger the baby.

She hated these men, Dalvetti and her father for every shot, for every drop of fear she felt with Gage putting his life on the line. But it only made her more determined to finish this once and for all.

The next shots shattered one of the windows in the bedroom. There was a window in the bathroom, as well, but it was on the back side of the place. Mason seemed to be positioned to stop anyone from making it back there.

She hoped.

But she also hoped that he wouldn't be hurt putting himself in harm's way for her.

The bullets started again and continued. Nonstop.

All of them aimed at Gage and the guesthouse. Several slammed into the trucks parked outside. One pinged against the rooster weather vane on the roof.

Mason leaned out from the tree and returned fire, a hail of bullets blasting through the air and into the fence.

Lynette had switched back to the screen with Gage when she saw the movement. Not the gunmen. But Patrick. He drew a gun from the back waist of his pants.

Oh, mercy. Was he going to try to shoot Gage? Lynette reached to press the button on the walkie-talkie to warn him, but Gage shouted something. Lynette couldn't hear what over the noise from the blasts, but Patrick froze.

The gunmen didn't.

One of them came up from the fence and took aim at Gage. Lynette wanted to scream for him to watch out, but he wouldn't hear her. Plus, the sound of her voice could be a distraction that could get him killed. Gage ducked down just in the nick of time, and the bullet went into the stone steps.

She watched, her breath in her throat, as one of the gunmen started running toward the guesthouse. He stayed low and dived back down when Mason sent a couple of shots his way.

Gage got up, positioned himself and took aim again with the rifle. He waited. And the moment the gunman reared his head again, Gage fired.

The gunman flew back, and Lynette saw the shock on his face before he hit the ground. If he wasn't dead, he soon would be, and Lynette felt nothing but relief.

One down. Two to go.

She didn't have to wait long for a second gunman to start firing. The shots bashed into the porch again and Gage thankfully dropped back down into cover.

How many times had he faced danger like this?

It sickened Lynette to think about it, especially since this sort of thing was probably part of his job description. It sickened her even more that she'd had a part in this. If she'd just managed to neutralize her father, he couldn't have done whatever he'd done to bring this killer literally to their doorsteps.

She touched the wedding ring that she'd put on her index finger. A poor substitute for Gage, but it calmed her a little. So did the prayers she said.

Suddenly, everything went quiet.

No shots. No sounds. Gage and the others seemed frozen, waiting.

Lynette waited, too, and kept praying that it was over. Her gaze flew over the screen, but she saw nothing. And for a few seconds, she thought maybe her prayers had been answered. Maybe the gunmen were dead.

But no.

The man reared up from the fence. No rifle this time. It was a big tube-looking device, and even though she'd never seen one, Lynette's first thought was that it was rocket launcher.

He aimed it at the guesthouse.

Now, she yelled for Gage to get down, and she turned, flattening her stomach against the tub. She braced herself for the blast that would likely rip the place, and maybe her, apart. But all she heard was another gunshot.

Her attention flew back to the screen.

And to Gage.

He had taken aim at the gunman, but the man and his rocket launcher were already tumbling to the ground.

Patrick, however, was standing, and it was his gun pointed in the direction of dead gunman number two.

Of all the ways Lynette had thought this would play

out, she hadn't expected Patrick to try to save them. If
that was indeed what he'd done.

More movement.

She saw the third man, the one she believed to be Dalvetti, running away. The man was in a full sprint.

Gage started to run, as well, and, with the rifle gripped
in his hand, he vaulted over the fence and raced after
the man.

Lynette wanted to hurry after Gage, to back him up,
but she knew that wouldn't help. Gage had told her to stay
put, and she would. Even if it was killing her to do that.

Some of the ranch hands followed Gage, but Mason
hurried to the front porch, positioning himself between
Patrick and the guesthouse. Probably because Mason
didn't trust Patrick. Or maybe he was worried Dalvetti
would circle back and come after her.

The seconds crawled by, and she had no idea how much
time passed. It seemed hours as she watched Gage run
after the man who'd just tried to kill them.

Soon, too soon, Gage disappeared from camera range.

It had been torture watching the gunfight, but it was
even worse now that she couldn't see Gage at all. Maybe
it was all the recent danger in her life, but her thoughts
ran wild, and she hoped that Gage would make it back
safely to her.

The front door opened, but Lynette could see that it
was Mason. "You okay?" he called out.

"Yes," she lied. She hadn't been hurt, but it would take
a lifetime or two to forget seeing those bullets come at
Gage like that.

"I killed him," Patrick called out to Mason. "Did you
see? I killed him."

"I saw," Mason answered. "I'll give you a gold star

later." Mason kept his attention fastened to the end of road where she'd last seen Gage.

Lynette watched both the road and Patrick. But thankfully Patrick still seemed to be on their side. Like Mason, he was caught up in watching the rest of this nightmare unfold.

She heard Mason curse, and there was nothing that could have prevented her from leaving the tub. Lynette raced to the door, praying that she wouldn't look out and see Gage wounded. Or worse.

It was Gage all right. And he was running back toward the house. Alone.

Gage cursed, too. "He got away."

Because her legs turned to rubber, she grabbed the door. Mason caught on to her.

"We'll get him," Mason promised her.

But she wasn't sure that was a promise Mason or anyone else could keep.

Gage jumped the fence and made it to her, barreling up the steps two at a time. He took over the duty of holding on to her, but he pulled her into his arms.

"We're leaving," he whispered. *"Now."*

He didn't say anything else. Gage took the Colt from her, stuffed it in the back waist of his jeans, and they hurried toward the bullet-riddled truck.

Chapter Thirteen

Gage parked the truck directly in front of the back entrance to the sheriff's office. After what had happened the last time they were here, he didn't want to take any chances, and he darn sure didn't want them to be out in the open any longer than necessary.

He hurried Lynette to the door that he knew would be unlocked, temporarily, because Gage had called ahead to arrange it. He didn't want anything slowing them down.

And he didn't want any more unnecessary risks.

There were no guarantees that Dalvetti wouldn't come after them here, but it was the safest place Gage could come up with on such short notice. It was a start, but he needed to make it as safe as possible for Lynette.

So he could go after Dalvetti and her father.

Gage was going to end this.

Now that he had the hall light to see her face, Gage gave Lynette a quick check. No signs of injury. Well, not physical ones anyway. But he didn't want to know what all this stress and danger were doing to her and the baby. He certainly wasn't dealing with it well. He wanted someone to pay and pay hard for this.

"Gage," he heard someone say at the exact moment he heard footsteps.

He looked up the hall and spotted his baby brother

Kade and a petite brunette with a rifle making their way toward them. Gage wasn't sure of the reaction he'd get. He had turned his back on his family ten years ago when he left town.

And on Lynette.

Now, he had some fences to mend if he wanted to get back into the fold.

He did want that, he realized.

Not just because he wanted family around for his child, but because he needed them.

Gage locked the door and walked closer, bracing himself for Kade's reaction. He'd spoken to Kade about unlocking the door, but it'd been a ten-second conversation at most. Too short to determine his brother's feelings about his return from the dead.

But Kade only smiled and pulled him into a long, hard hug.

"Glad you're back," Kade whispered. "Wish it were under better circumstances."

"Me, too," Gage agreed.

Kade pulled back, stepped to the side and eased his arm around the brunette's shoulder. "My wife, Bree. Bree, this is your other brother-in-law, Gage."

Bree smiled. "I have a lot of them." She shook Gage's hand with a grip a lot firmer than he'd expected from someone who barely came up to his shoulder, and then she looked at Lynette. "Are you doing okay?"

Lynette gave a hollow laugh. "Been better."

"Yes, I heard. Mason called, told us all about it. A shoot-out with a drug kingpin isn't my idea of a restful evening, either."

Gage could attest firsthand that was true.

"How are the twins—Leah and Mia?" Lynette asked

Bree, making Gage realize that she had kept in touch with his family. Or at least kept up with the gossip.

Bree nodded. "They're good. Growing like weeds and probably giving the nanny some gray hairs because they're still not sleeping through the night." Bree combed her gaze over Gage. "You can tell you're a Ryland. You look like the rest of them. I'm betting you're as hard-headed, too."

"Oh, he is. The worst of the lot." Kade flexed his eyebrows and managed a thin smile. A smile that quickly faded. "Nate's on the way here. You haven't seen Dade or him yet."

Gage shook his head. "But I don't want them here if it means putting the rest of the family in danger. They have wives and kids to protect."

"We're working on that," Kade assured him. "Grayson's at the hospital with Eve. She's still in labor."

"Might be a long one," Bree added in a mumble.

Gage silently cursed Dalvetti and Ford again. Lynette and he should be at the hospital, happily awaiting the birth of Grayson's firstborn, but instead they were on the run for their lives. And maybe putting others in danger by being in danger themselves.

"Dade's in San Antonio with the others," Kade continued. "But SAPD, Nate's men, will take over security detail when Dade comes here."

So, the plan was for him to have four brothers and a very capable-looking sister-in-law for backup.

Gage wasn't going to refuse any of their help.

Lynette came first, and that meant swallowing his fears about their safety. Plus, there was the fact that he didn't trust anyone as much as he trusted his siblings.

"Darcy dropped by earlier," Bree explained, looking at Lynette now. "She brought you some clothes and toiletries that she got from your house. Your cell phone, too. Darcy wasn't sure which clothes to pack so she just got some things from your closet and drawers."

"Whatever she brought will be fine, I'm sure. I'll thank her the next time I see her."

Bree hitched her thumb to the stairs. "There's an apartment you can use to get some rest and a shower if you want. It's not much more than a flop room, but no one is going to get in this place to come after you."

"Bree's former FBI," Kade supplied. "And both of us have sniper training."

That might come in handy, and it was a reminder that Bree obviously fit well into the family. Kade had done good.

"If it comes down to needing long-range shooters," Kade continued, "we can use me and Bree." But then he huffed. "Even though I'd prefer Bree not be in the line of fire."

Bree came up on her toes and kissed him. "I can take care of myself."

"I'd rather not risk it."

Gage understood that, too. And he wouldn't take the chance, either. It was obvious his kid brother was crazy in love, and it would make Kade just plain crazy if he knew his wife's life was at more risk than necessary. He'd work it so Bree was on protection detail for Lynette. Neither woman would probably like that much, but he didn't want them on the front lines.

"Too bad Patrick's not a suspect," Lynette mumbled.

Yeah, too bad. "Patrick took out one of Dalvetti's men," Gage explained.

That seemed to surprise Kade as much as it had surprised Gage. "You think that means Patrick's not behind any of this?" Kade asked.

Gage shook his head. "I'm not sure. Heck, Patrick could have set up that entire attack and then killed the gunman just to take blame off himself."

Kade and Bree made sounds of agreement. Lynette, too. So, Patrick was still on their short list of suspects despite having done them a favor. That list wasn't getting any shorter, and it might be a while before they could eliminate a name or two.

"I just want this to end," Lynette said. Gage heard the fatigue and knew the adrenaline crash was coming. He was sure feeling it.

"It will," Kade promised her. He gave Lynette's arm a gentle squeeze. "This is our fight now, too."

So, four brothers and a sister. But even that didn't mean good odds. "Sampson Dalvetti is rich and ruthless. He won't come alone. He's probably regrouping right now and assembling a new team of assassins."

"I read his file," Kade said. "He's not stupid, either, and that means he probably won't come here gunning for trouble. Not in the middle of town."

Gage hoped that was true, but he wasn't going to base Lynette's safety on hope. No. He had to get Lynette settled into the apartment, make a few more security arrangements, and then he needed to call her father.

Something Gage didn't intend to tell Lynette.

There was a knock at the front door, and all of them turned in that direction. All of them groaned. Gage and Kade cursed, as well.

"I'll get rid of her," Kade mumbled, and he headed toward the glass door where Gage could see Nicole waiting and knocking again.

"You think she got that court order to put me back in the loony bin?" Lynette asked.

Gage shrugged and tried to give Lynette a reassuring

glance. When that didn't work, he kissed her, and then followed Bree and his brother.

Apparently, this long-assed day wasn't over yet.

"Why don't you wait upstairs in the apartment?" Gage suggested to Lynette. But as expected, she went with him to the front door.

And he couldn't blame her. Nicole was trying to railroad her, and Gage could understand Lynette's need to face down the woman.

Kade unlocked the door but used his body to block Nicole from coming in. "What do you want?" he snarled.

"Your help." Nicole's voice didn't sound any steadier than Lynette's.

Nicole looked past Kade, and her attention landed on Lynette. "I need your help, too."

"Really?" Lynette challenged. She folded her arms over her chest. "With what? You want me to have myself committed to the asylum so it'll cut down on the time you're spending on this witch hunt?"

"No. That *witch hunt* is over. On my part anyway. I can't say the same for your father or Patrick."

"Patrick?" Lynette challenged. "So, now he'll try to have me committed?"

Nicole groaned softly and shoved her perfectly styled hair from her perfectly made-up face. "I don't know what Patrick will try to do. Kill you, maybe. Because he believes you're trying to send him to jail."

"We are," Gage volunteered. "If he's done anything that warrants jail. Did he?"

For a moment Gage thought she might answer, but Nicole only shook her head. "I have enough enemies without making one of Patrick." She looked at Lynette again. "I'm here because of your father." She paused a heartbeat. "Ford knows."

Nicole dropped her gaze to Lynette's stomach.

And to the baby.

"Ford knows," Nicole repeated.

KADE AND BREE LOOKED at Lynette, and they obviously wanted an explanation about what the heck was going on.

Lynette wanted the same thing.

Gage kept his right hand over his gun, but he moved closer to her, until they were shoulder to shoulder. And he waited just as Lynette did, because she wasn't about to volunteer anything to Nicole. This could be a fishing expedition.

"Ford knows you're pregnant," Nicole clarified.

So, no fishing expedition. Lynette pulled in her breath and wondered just how bad things would get now. Pretty bad. Because this would only enrage her father even more, and it might even explain why Dalvetti had attacked them.

"You're pregnant?" Kade asked.

Lynette nodded.

"It's Gage's baby," Nicole supplied. "Ford knows that, too."

Gage stared at Nicole. "Am I supposed to care a rat's butt that my spit wad of a father-in-law knows my wife is pregnant?" Gage glanced at his brother. "Yeah, Lynette and I are still married. Long story."

"I didn't get the annulment," Lynette volunteered.

Gage shrugged. "So, maybe not so long after all." He turned back to Nicole. "Did you think I'd be shaking in my boots? Well, I'm not. And if Ford sent you here—"

"He didn't," Nicole interrupted.

"Then why the heck are you here?" Gage demanded.

Nicole looked away, mumbled something that Lynette didn't catch. "Ford blackmailed me into starting the paperwork to have Lynette committed. I, uh, did some things. Things that Ford said Lynette found when she was investigating me."

Lynette shook her head. "I found nothing, and you're only implicating yourself by coming here like this."

"I had to warn you," Nicole countered.

Gage gave the woman a skeptical look that Lynette was certain matched hers. She was even more skeptical because Patrick had come to the guesthouse to make a similar whine, and it had been the start of Dalvetti's attack.

"It's true. I'm trying to help you," Nicole insisted. "All I ask in return is immunity if any charges are filed against me."

Sheesh. Another immunity deal. Both Patrick and Nicole must think she'd dug up some pretty smelly dirt for them to react this way.

"No deal," Gage assured Nicole.

Lynette mumbled an agreement. She'd had enough from all the vipers involved, or potentially involved, in this. "If you don't mind, Gage and I will decline your *help*."

"Fine," Nicole snapped. But she didn't budge. Her red-lacquered mouth tightened into a fine line.

"If there's nothing else…" Gage prompted. He nudged Lynette to get moving.

"Wait!" Nicole called out.

Lynette and Gage did, but it took several seconds for Nicole to continue. "About a year ago, Ford had a tracking device put on your car. When you went to San Antonio to see that doctor, it only took Ford about an hour to bribe him into telling him what you were up to."

Lynette cursed the fear that coiled through her, and then she cursed that her father had violated every moment of her privacy. She didn't want him having even a thought of her precious baby in his monstrous mind.

"Ford didn't think you'd go through with the insemination," Nicole added. "He thought you'd realize how much he hates Gage and do the right thing."

Lynette met her eye to eye. "I did the right thing." And since she was as tired of the fear as she was this conversation, she turned again to go to the apartment.

"Ford brought that drug dealer here," Nicole called out.

That stopped Lynette, only because it stopped Gage. Lynette wondered if Nicole was aware that Patrick had made the same accusation.

"What do you know about Dalvetti?" Gage pressed.

Nicole drew in a weary breath. "I know Ford would do anything to get you out of Lynette's life."

Gage lifted his shoulder. "Hard to do that now that she's carrying my baby."

Now, Nicole swallowed hard. Maybe faked. Maybe real. She also glanced away from them. "Ford has no intentions of letting this baby arrive into the world."

The rage that went through her was instant. Gage tried to catch on to her, but Lynette scrambled over the reception counter. She latched on to Nicole and slammed her against the glass door.

Lynette tried to speak, to yell, scream, anything, but the words couldn't make it through her clamped throat. How dare her father threaten her child.

Gage eased her away from Nicole, but then he got in the woman's face. "Tell Ford I'll deal with him soon."

The fury in Gage's voice was nothing compared to the look he shot Nicole. The woman gave a shaky nod and hurried out the door.

Lynette stood there, watching Nicole scurry away.

Oh, God.

She could feel the showdown coming. And Lynette prayed that Gage wouldn't die trying to protect their child.

Chapter Fourteen

Gage glanced around the apartment above the sheriff's office to see if he'd done everything to make it as safe as possible.

He'd pulled down the blinds. No lights were on. The door was locked. He had two guns, a rifle, and the windows were rigged with security sensors that would alert them if anyone tried to break in. He had a cell phone, walkie-talkie and a landline phone.

Of course, the best security measures were downstairs.

Mason, Dade, Nate, Kade and Bree.

The Rylands were on duty. Or as Mason always liked to say "justice isn't just coming—it's already here." Gage was counting heavily on that to get them through this night.

Gage glanced around the apartment again. Double-checking. He couldn't see anything that needed correction. Now, all that was left was to make Lynette get some rest. That might not be easy since she was watching him like a hawk. No doubt worried that he'd go off half-cocked to confront her father about the threat he'd made to the baby.

And he *would* confront Ford.

Gage just wouldn't do it half-cocked though.

No, it was best to do these things with a cool head.

Hopefully, he could choke down his anger and do that. But Gage was actually looking forward to beating some sense into Ford even if there would be consequences to pay for that.

"You didn't eat much," Lynette told him.

She was seated on the sofa finishing off one of the sandwiches Nate had brought. Gage had had to play dirty again when she'd at first said she wasn't hungry. He'd asked her to eat for the baby's sake.

And she had.

Not just the sandwich but some milk and an apple. He made a mental note to use that trick again if necessary.

"I'll eat more later," he promised. But right now, he felt like a wet gym bag, and this might be the only lull he got to wash off some of the grime from the earlier attack. He took his grandfather's Colt from the back waist of his jeans and put it on the countertop of the makeshift kitchen. "I need to grab a shower."

Gage hadn't tossed that out there without thinking it through. He knew it couldn't be just a shower. Because there was no way he would leave Lynette in the room alone. Of course, he could get one of his brothers to sit with her, but he preferred them doing guard duty downstairs so that all the windows and doors were covered.

"You'll have to come in the bathroom with me while I shower," he said.

She stood, slowly, and even in the dim light he saw her turn toward him. Also slowly. She was staring at him. He could feel it.

And he could also feel the air drain right out of the room.

"Are you keeping on your clothes for that?" she asked.

He gave her a scowl that she couldn't see, but she no

doubt knew it was there. "No," he mumbled. "And that should make things interesting, huh?"

"Not if I can't see you," she mumbled back.

Oh, yeah. This was going to be torture. But necessary. When he told her the part about his going after her father, Gage would want to pull her into his arms. To steady her, and to steady himself. He didn't want her keeling over from the smell of gunshot residue, sweat and mud.

Even if a shower could lead to things best left alone.

He walked ahead of her into the tiny bathroom. Since there was only one small window, it was even darker than the main room, and Gage intended for it to stay that way. He didn't want to risk that someone could use the lights to target them with a long-range rifle. And he had firsthand knowledge that Dalvetti liked to arm his goons with rifles.

The rocket launcher had been a surprise though.

Gage hadn't heard of the man using one before. Maybe that had been Ford's little contribution to the assault. But Ford, Dalvetti or his men hopefully wouldn't get close enough to the sheriff's office to use a weapon like that. That's because Mason had set up barricades that blocked off streets on all sides. Plus, one of Kade's coworkers and Kade were on the roof with sniper rifles. If Dalvetti tried to get near the place, he'd be stopped. For good.

"Stay put," he warned Lynette when she was in the doorway of the bathroom. "I'll hurry."

He stripped down, fully aware that she didn't take her attention off him. Heck, he would have done the same if she'd been the one going bare. In fact, maybe he could reverse it when he was done. Seeing Lynette naked would make him feel a whole lot better.

For a few seconds anyway.

And then that good feeling would lead to sex. As much as Gage wanted that—and he wanted it bad—he wasn't sure she needed him inside her while she was going through all this emotional turmoil.

"You got a tattoo," Lynette commented. She sank down onto the floor, her back against the closed door.

Obviously, the room wasn't as dark as he thought.

"Yeah." A heart with a dagger through it on his right shoulder. "I was pretty mad about that annulment I thought you got."

She laughed, and the sound rippled through him.

Gage mentally cursed, threw back the shower curtain and turned the water on as hot as it would go. He probably should have chosen cold, but he was already sure he was fighting a losing battle here.

He took his time, lathered up twice, rinsed and re-rinsed, hoping that exhaustion would cause Lynette to fall asleep—something both the baby and she needed. He needed it for them, too, so it would give him one less thing to worry about. But when Gage turned off the water and opened the curtain back up, Lynette wasn't asleep.

She was staring at him.

Correction: she was *waiting* for him.

Gage knew her well enough to know the difference.

He waited, too, hoping that sanity and common sense would kick in.

Nope, they didn't.

He had the willpower of a termite on wood when it came to Lynette.

"You're sure you're up for this?" he clarified.

"I'm not the one who needs to be up." And she chuckled again.

Gage groaned.

Yes, this would be a special kind of sweet torture.

He grabbed a towel, dried his face and stepped from

the tub. The two-second debate he intended to have with himself didn't even last that long. A split second, tops.

"Let's just go for it," she whispered, "and we'll work out the rest later."

There was no way he could refuse that, especially since he'd already reached the same conclusion. "Deal," he agreed.

Dripping wet and already burning for her, he hooked the towel around the back of her neck, dropped down and pulled her to him. Everything happened fast. Like a train wreck.

Like a fantasy.

His mouth took hers, and the thoughts in his head, and the doubts, turned to ash.

"Gage," she whispered.

That got through the ash, and he realized that his name coming from her lips was what he wanted most.

Well, one of the things he wanted anyway.

He amped up the kiss, letting himself savor the taste of her. Man, he'd missed her. His body had been with other women—something he'd keep to himself—but in his mind, he'd only ever made love to Lynette. Even when he hated her, or believed he did, he couldn't stop himself from thinking of her.

And now, he didn't have to think.

He was with her again.

Good thing, too, because she dropped some kisses on his neck that created more ash in his brain. She didn't stop there. Lynette coiled her warm arms around him and pulled him closer until she was pressed against him and it was impossible to tell where her body ended and his began.

The kiss got hotter and hungrier in a hurry.

Lynette and he could never just keep things simple.

They kissed until they finally had to break for air or suffocate. They gasped for breath and then went right back at each other. A kissing battle, raging. But as he could have predicted, kisses only made his body want more.

He did *more*.

Gage slid his hand up her top and touched her breasts. She was perfect. Small and soft. He got the reaction he wanted— She made a breathy moan and climbed into his lap with her sex aligned right against his. It was good. Old memories slammed with new ones that they were about to make.

But it wasn't enough.

He needed her naked, and he needed to be inside her. Gage stripped off her top. Her bra. And kissed her the way he wanted to kiss her.

She made another breathy moan.

And she did some touching of her own. Her hand dallied on his chest, pecking at the coils of hair there, but then she moved downward. To his stomach.

Oh, man.

He'd forgotten that she knew all his hot spots. Those all-knowing fingers went down his stomach and to pay-dirt territory. She wrapped her fingers around his erection.

That sped things up. After he got his eyes uncrossed, that is.

Gage considered taking her into the other room and to the bed, but he doubted they'd make it there. Since they were already on the floor, that'd have to do.

Lynette had the same idea because without breaking the kiss, she started to lower herself onto the floor.

"No deal. The floor's hard and cold," he reminded her. "It'll leave tile marks on your butt."

She chuckled, but there was a nervous edge to it. "Then figure out something fast."

He did.

Gage turned her, putting her back against the door again, and he yanked off those loose sweatpants and panties so her butt was on the rug, not the tile.

Naked, finally.

There were no more obstacles. He fastened her legs around his waist and lifted her back onto his lap.

Gage kept kissing her and wanted to apologize for the short foreplay, but it was clear she didn't want foreplay any more than he did. She drew back her hand, and Gage pushed into her.

His head exploded.

Thank goodness other parts of him didn't do the same.

But it was a challenge. She was made for him. Made to send jolts of pleasure through every inch of him. Maybe Lynette felt the same about him, because she stilled for a moment.

He heard a sound he didn't want to hear.

And he froze. "You're crying?"

"Good crying," she assured him. "I've missed you more... Well, just more."

Gage held his breath, waiting.

"I'll respect you in the morning," she added.

He might have smiled at her joke if she didn't start moving, her hips pushing forward to take him deeper inside her. Gage tried to keep things gentle. He caught on to her hips, to set the pace and slow things down.

That didn't work, either.

Her mouth came to his, and she smothered him with one of those scalding-hot French kisses. *Slow down* went out the window. Taking her was all that mattered now. Finishing this.

Finishing *her*.

Gage slid his hand between their bodies, to add some touches to the now frantic strokes. It wouldn't take much. He knew as much about her hot buttons as she knew about his. That's why she took that kiss to his neck.

Yeah.

More pay dirt.

Gage felt his vision blur but kept touching her. Even when she shattered around him, he touched her.

He kissed her.

Lynette's mouth was on his when he gathered her into his arms. And Gage let himself fall fast and hard.

Chapter Fifteen

Other than the bad timing, Lynette had no regrets about having sex with Gage. She'd waited a long time to be back in his arms, and she would deal with the regrets later.

Especially one.

She didn't want Gage to feel trapped in the life she had created for herself. A life with a baby. There probably weren't any CIA assignments nearby in Silver Creek, which meant, well, he could feel trapped.

Of course, she didn't want him trapped in her backup plan, either. That's what the condo in Dallas was all about. She'd already created a fake identity and arranged for a job there so she could keep her pregnancy and baby from her father. With that cat now out of the proverbial bag, she wasn't sure where she should go. Or what she should do. But she didn't want Gage caught up in this unless it was what he wanted with all his heart and soul.

She'd seen no signs of that.

Yes, he wanted her. Her body. Even the baby. But she wasn't sure he'd gotten past what had happened all those years ago. She certainly wasn't sure he loved her.

Later, once she'd caught her breath and he'd caught his, she'd give him an out. And she had to brace herself in case he jumped at the chance to take it. Ten years was a long time, and she might not know this Gage as well as she'd known the kid who had proposed to her all those years ago.

Gage scooped her up off the floor, and with them both stark naked, he walked into the main room and deposited her on the bed. But not before giving her one of those mind-numbing kisses to make her head fuzzy again and her body hot.

"Don't get dressed yet," she whispered when he started back toward the bathroom where he'd left his clothes. Hers, too.

"My brothers will be here soon," he reminded her. "I need to go over the security plans with them and make sure every inch of the place is protected."

All that was necessary, but it would also be a reunion, the first time they'd been together in years. Lynette figured they had some catching up to do.

"Give me a minute." And she pulled him onto the bed with her.

Yes. That was her body's first reaction. She'd just had Gage, literally, but holding him naked like this was almost as good as the sex.

Almost.

She ran her hands over his chest and to his back, where those corded muscles responded to her touch. And then her hands went lower.

"Playing?" he teased.

"Remembering," she countered.

She put her face against the curve of his neck and took in his musky male scent. Oh, mercy. It was the best kind of memory. That scent had her numb, and just like that she was ready for him all over again.

Gage did some playing of his own. He pushed her hair aside, his fingers lingering on her face.

"You should come with a warning label," he said, repeating what she'd told him earlier. "Dangerous curves ahead."

She laughed, and it felt so good to be in this moment with Gage. But the moment couldn't last. Both knew it. And that's why he kissed her again.

"When this is over, we'll talk," he assured her. He didn't elaborate or even mention the subject. Didn't have to. He wanted to have an *us* talk, and she needed to have an *out* talk. She feared both.

"Maybe we'll even do more of this," Gage added.

More of this sounded perfect and made Lynette want to delay the talk for months and months because it might lead to Gage leaving again.

"My brothers," he reminded her, and he left her to get his clothes. "You stay put, though. I want you and the baby to get some rest."

She needed rest. There was no denying that, but she had no intentions of being naked in bed when his brothers stopped by to see him.

"Bring me back my bra," she reminded him. She didn't want her ring to fall out and get lost.

"Bra detail," he joked. "My favorite."

Lynette gave a weary sigh, got up, as well, and in the murky light she located the overnight bag that Darcy had packed for her. Even though she couldn't actually see the jeans, top and underwear, she put them on and welcomed the clean clothes.

Her cell phone, too.

Lynette turned it on and saw the eleven missed calls from her father. He'd left voice mails, too, but she didn't even bother with them.

"Rest," Gage repeated when he came out of the bathroom. He put her bra in the overnight bag. And to make sure that *rest* would happen, he picked her up again, put her back in bed and draped the comforter over her.

"I'd rest better with you."

"You wouldn't rest at all with me." He kissed her again. "I'm staying close, on the stairs, and I'll leave the door open so I can see you. Sleep," he insisted. "Tomorrow, we'll work out what we're going to do about Dalvetti."

Maybe by then this fuzzy haze wouldn't be clouding her head. Heck, while she was hoping, maybe Dalvetti and her father would wipe each other off the face of the earth.

Lynette watched through the murkiness as Gage walked away from her and to the door. When he opened it, she could just make out the others who were already there. Four of his brothers—Nate, Dade, Kade and Mason. Nate and Dade hugged him. Spoke in whispers. And Gage eased the door partially shut, so that she could see only him.

And he could see her.

She tried to listen to what they were saying. There was a lot of catching up to do, and she wondered if Gage would tell his brothers that he was still married to her and that they had a baby on the way. Lynette also wondered if he would tell them how he felt about her.

Because he sure as heck hadn't told her.

With that thought she drew in an exhausted breath, and even though she fought it, Lynette couldn't keep her eyelids from drifting down.

She fell asleep with the taste of Gage's kisses still on her lips.

GAGE WAITED until he was sure Lynette was asleep. His brothers were waiting for that, too, even though he hadn't actually said that there were things he preferred that Lynette didn't hear.

Things she wasn't going to like.

"Lynette's pregnant," Gage said in case one of them hadn't gotten the word. Apparently, they had. Later, he'd explain how the pregnancy had come about, but that could wait. "If this danger continues, I'm worried she could lose the baby." He was more worried that he could lose her.

"So, what's the plan?" Dade asked without hesitation.

That put a lump in Gage's throat. It'd been a while since someone had had his back like this. "I'm starting with Ford Herrington. He's a killer, plain and simple, and he's not going to stop until someone dies. I'm sure that I'm on top of his to-murder list, but he's brought Lynette into this, and it has to stop."

"A showdown," Nate concurred. "How? When? What do you need from us?"

"I need Lynette protected first." Gage looked at Mason, who had his back against the stairwell wall, his feet crossed at the ankles. Then Nate. Then Dade. "I need you to stay here and make sure no one gets to her."

"Bree can give Mason some backup," Kade suggested. "Both deputies, too."

Gage nodded. No doubt Kade wanted that so he could keep his wife out of direct harm's way. Gage understood that completely. But even with six lawmen guarding Lynette, he worried it might not be enough.

"Call in anyone you trust from the ranch," Gage continued. "I can't use my people because there might be some kind of leak in communication. But I want to make this building a fortress, and that includes more people on the roof who can stop a sniper or rocket launcher attack."

All of them nodded.

Kade turned to him. "And what will I be doing?"

"You'll be here, too, and keeping a safe distance from

me," Gage assured him. "I have no plans to make Bree a widow."

"Sounds like you're planning to make Lynette one," Mason growled. "If Kade keeps a safe distance from you, that means you're pretty much going in somewhere alone."

Gage couldn't disagree with that. "I'll call Ford and arrange a meeting at the city hall building. Before I make the call, Mason and I will already be in place there, and Mason will be on the roof watching in case Ford tries to pull something."

"Ford *will* try to pull something," Nate spoke up.

Still no argument from Gage. "I don't want to take any more of you away from this building. Lynette comes first, understand?"

"So, you're just going to meet with Ford and have a nice friendly chat?" Mason asked, and he didn't bother to take out the snark.

Now, Gage could disagree. "It won't be friendly. But one way or another the danger from him stops tonight. Then, in the morning I can deal with Dalvetti—*alone,*" Gage added before any of them could ask.

"Last I heard there was no *I* in team or brothers," Mason mumbled.

"I can't risk your lives."

"To hell you can't," Mason fired back. He stooped down so they were all eye level. "You want to stop Ford Herrington tonight, then put us all to good use. Together, we can stop him."

Gage stood, shook his head. "Protect Lynette," he repeated.

He didn't wait for their assurances. Didn't need them. They might not agree with his plan, but they would do it. And right now, keeping Lynette and his baby alive was the only thing that mattered.

Chapter Sixteen

The beeping sound woke Lynette. She sat up in the bed and automatically reached for Gage, only to remember that he wasn't there. He was with his brothers.

Lynette tried to settle her breathing. Her stomach, too, since the sudden movement had caused a wave of nausea to come over her. She prayed this wasn't the start of a bout of morning sickness, because the timing sucked. There were already too many things on Gage's and her minds.

She heard the beep again, and this time she realized it was her cell phone, letting her know that she had another voice mail. Lynette glanced at the clock. It was nearly midnight. And there was only one person who'd call her at this hour.

Her father.

And she didn't want to speak to him.

She threw back the covers and looked around. Listened, too. She could no longer hear the whispered conversations on the stairwell. That caused her to jump from the bed, and despite the sick feeling in her stomach, she hurried to the ajar door.

No one was on the stairs.

And the place was way too quiet.

Except for her phone. It beeped again.

Lynette grabbed the cell from the bag and jammed

the button to retrieve her calls, and she quickly learned that she'd been right. It was her father. She pressed another button to listen to the message that he'd left just seconds earlier.

"I'm meeting with Gage at the courthouse in ten minutes," her father's recorded voice said. "Call me now."

Oh, God.

Lynette's hands started to shake, but somehow she managed to return the call. "What have you done?" she asked the second he answered.

"Nothing. Not yet anyway. Gage called me earlier and set up a meeting at the courthouse. I got the distinct impression he was going to try to kill me."

No. Gage couldn't arrange a meeting like this behind her back. It wasn't just dangerous. It could be suicide.

"I'm assuming no one else is listening in on this call, but just in case, I'll mince words."

A veiled threat was no doubt coming, and Lynette tried to brace herself for it. What she wanted to do was reach through the phone and tear her father to shreds. But for now her best bet was to listen to what Gage and he had done and then try to figure out how to keep Gage alive.

"Gage and I are going to *talk*," her father said. There it was, the veiled threat. "If you don't come, too, then you'll be very sorry. You could lose the things that matter most to you. And Gage, well, Gage could lose a lot more than that."

His words fired through her and nearly brought Lynette to her knees.

"If you call Gage to warn him," her father continued, "then it'll only make things worse. I'll see you in a few minutes. Oh, and, Lynette, this would be a good time to obey your father."

Lynette slapped the phone shut, hurriedly put on her

shoes and grabbed the gun that Gage had left for her on the dresser. She ran down the steps, praying that her father had been lying and that she'd find all the Rylands there.

She didn't.

No one was in any of the offices that she raced past, and the lights had all been turned out. Something was wrong.

"Gage?" she called out.

"Stay there," someone answered. Not Gage. But Kade. He came out from the pitch-black reception area by the front door, and he made his way down the hall toward her.

"Where's Gage?" she asked, and she felt the terror crawling up her spine.

That feeling only got worse when Kade didn't answer right away. "He's meeting with your father."

Oh, mercy. The call wasn't a hoax. Her father had managed to set up what she'd thought would be impossible. "It's a trap. My father just called and said if I didn't show up at the courthouse that I could lose Gage. I have to go to that meeting."

Kade shook his head. "Gage's orders are for you to stay put. Don't worry," Kade added. "We've covered the entire place. Nate, Bree and some other FBI agents are on the roof. Dade is guarding the back of the building. Dalvetti and his men can't get within a quarter of a mile of this place without us knowing."

"But I could tell by the way he was talking that my father intends to kill Gage at the courthouse."

Kade caught on to her arm to keep her from bolting. "Gage has everything set up. Some of the ranch hands are watching the courthouse to make sure Ford doesn't pull anything. And Mason is there, too. He's on the roof of the adjacent building."

It wasn't enough. Not nearly enough. "Gage went in alone to that meeting?"

Kade didn't answer. He didn't have to. Because she knew that's exactly what Gage had done.

"I have to help him," Lynette insisted.

"You can't. Gage wants you to stay here."

Lynette threw off his grip and got right in Kade's face. "I'm not asking for your permission. I'm helping Gage, period."

She started down the hall toward the back exit, but Kade raced after her. He took her arm again and whirled her around.

"Gage said I was to tell you to think of the baby," Kade warned. "You can't put the baby in danger."

It took a moment for Lynette to steady her voice so she could speak. "I won't endanger the baby. I'll do everything to stay safe, but I have to help. I can't lose Gage. Not again." She stared at him, even though she could barely see his face. "Please."

"I can't let you go," he argued.

Lynette couldn't outmuscle him, and even though she hated to pull her gun on him, she would if it came down to it. Of course, Kade probably knew that she had no intention of shooting him. Her only intention now was to get to Gage in time to save him from her father.

"Please," Lynette repeated. "What if it were Bree out there instead of Gage?"

Another pause. Then Kade cursed. "But Gage will throttle me if I let you go."

"You're not letting me go. I'm doing this on my own."

She remembered seeing a jacket in Grayson's office so she hurried there to get it. Not for the warmth but so she could slip the gun in the pocket. She didn't want to go running up Main Street brandishing a Colt .45. Lynette located a raincoat, some extra ammunition, and then she spotted the tiny tape recorder on Grayson's desk.

It was a long shot, and it certainly hadn't worked in the past, but it might come in handy.

"Reconsider this," Kade warned her.

"No." And she didn't even have to think about her answer. She ran to the back exit and prayed she would get to Gage in time.

FORD HERRINGTON WAS LATE.

Gage checked his watch again and cursed. When he'd called Ford nearly two hours ago, the man had assured Gage that he was *eager* for them to talk.

Right.

More like Ford was eager to try to finish Gage off.

But that was all right. Gage didn't care why Lynette's father had agreed to meet with him, he was just glad all of this was about to come to a head.

"See anything?" Gage asked Mason through the walkie-talkie. Mason and two of his ranch hands were on the roof. Waiting. Just like Gage.

"Nothing other than Herman Smith staggering home drunk. All okay down there?"

"Peachy," Gage mumbled, and he clicked the button to end the conversation so he could keep watch around him.

The lobby of the courthouse wasn't exactly sprawling, but it had a curved staircase feeding off one side and a wide hall off the other. Plus, there were the doors and windows. It did have one big bonus though— It was surrounded on all four sides by parking lots and the street, and there wasn't a vehicle out there now that he had sent the night watchman home.

Neither Dalvetti nor Ford would make it across those open spaces without Mason or the ranch hands spotting them—especially since Gage was betting neither would come alone.

Another bonus to the courthouse was there were no convenient nearby buildings where gunmen could hide. Lynette's one-story newspaper office was on the left side. It was locked up, and he'd seen the red light blinking on the activated security alarm when he'd looked in the window.

On the front and back side of the courthouse were streets that Mason had blocked off. Someone could perhaps get through the barricade by ramming into it, but it would take a big vehicle and a determined driver.

That left the right side where there was a hotel under construction. Unfortunately, there were places to hide inside, which was why one of the ranch hands had specific orders to keep his eyes on it at all times.

Gage checked the time again. Cursed some more. And he thought of Lynette. Of how just hours earlier he'd taken her hard and fast on the bathroom floor. Hardly romantic. He owed her something better.

Hell, he owed her something better than him.

He truly had been trouble for her, and he wasn't sure he could give her the normal, quiet life that she craved.

"Incoming," Mason said over the walkie-talkie. "It's Ford, and he has two goons with him."

Gage immediately pushed aside the thoughts of Lynette, took a deep breath and readied himself. "I'll let them in."

"All of them?" Mason questioned.

"Yeah, I'll be careful." Gage cut off whatever Mason was about to argue, and clipped the walkie-talkie to his belt so his hands would be free.

He went to the front door, unlocked it and then stepped back into the shadows at the edge of the hall. There was a gun in his right hand, another in the back waist of his jeans, and his jacket pocket was crammed with extra ammunition. He wasn't much for wearing Kevlar, but for this meeting Gage had made an exception and borrowed one from Grayson's office.

Ford had killed at least once, and Gage was betting that his goons and he wouldn't hesitate to kill again.

One of the goons came in first with his gun already drawn. Then Ford, followed by the third man holding a weapon. All wore dark clothes and stayed by the door. The guards looked around, probably trying to figure out the best place to take cover if shots were fired.

But there wasn't any cover.

It was another reason Gage had picked this place. If it came down to it, he could dive into the hall. Not exactly out of the line of fire, but it was better than trying to get back out that door.

Of course, he was outnumbered three to one.

"Check for bugs," Ford ordered the men. One stayed by him, but the other pulled a handheld device from his pocket. A transmitter detector. And he began to prowl around the room.

"What about Ryland's walkie-talkie?" one of the men asked.

Gage glanced down at it. "You want it? Come and get it."

"Hold off on that," Ford told his men. "He has some hand-to-hand combat skills, and I don't want to give him the opportunity to use them on you. Besides, no one on the other end of the walkie-talkie can hear what we're saying unless Gage pushes the button. He won't do that if he wants this meeting to continue."

Yeah, Gage wanted it to continue. And end. With Ford out of the picture one way or another.

"Gage," Ford repeated like profanity. "You've come to make a deal with me."

"I have." Best to keep this simple. "I want you to back off and leave Lynette alone."

"I can't," Ford quickly answered. "She has to pay for her disobedience. Imagine, my own daughter doing that. My only blood kin. I'm sure you know how painful something like would be."

Gage figured that could be a reference to the baby. Maybe even a cleverly worded threat. But he didn't bite. Not yet anyway.

"Look, we both know you're dirty," Gage continued, "but Lynette isn't going to look for proof of that. She stopped her investigation."

His bug-searching goon gave Ford a thumbs-up. "No one's listening but us."

Ford smiled then shook his head. "Lynette stopped her investigation too late."

"It's never too late," Gage countered.

Another headshake. "You seem to believe I have complete control over all of this. I don't. Patrick and Nicole are shaken up, too, and if one of them believes Lynette found anything incriminating, they'd be willing to do something about it. So, you see, I'm not the only person who might want to stop my daughter."

"She didn't find anything," Gage supplied.

"They think she's lying." Ford paused. "Lynette stopped digging for one reason— She decided that she wanted to test-drive motherhood. But I'm betting she found plenty before she got pregnant with your bastard child."

Okay, that chipped away at the temper that Gage was trying to keep in check. "Not a bastard," Gage calmly corrected. "Lynette and I are still married."

"An abomination of a marriage. That makes your baby an abomination, too."

"No, it makes this baby a Ryland." Gage huffed. "Are you trying to make me want to kill you? Because that's not necessary. I already want you dead."

There was just enough light that Gage saw Ford smile again. He motioned for his men to stay put, and he started toward Gage. Gage didn't aim his weapon at the man, not exactly, but he kept it ready just in case.

"Then go ahead." Ford came closer. Closer. And stopped just a few feet away. He outstretched his arms. "Shoot me. Right here, right now."

It wasn't even tempting. Okay, it was. But just briefly. "Pull first and I will."

"Chicken?" Ford taunted.

"Sane," Gage taunted back. "Can you say the same? And before you answer that, remember you killed your wife, had your daughter committed to the loony bin, spied on her, had her stalked. And now you want her dead."

All traces of Ford's smile vanished. "I never wanted Lynette dead. I just wanted a daughter who would love and respect me."

Gage wondered if Ford really wanted that or if he was just blowing smoke. "Committing multiple felonies is not the way to get love and respect."

"I'll never admit to those things," Ford snapped. "I don't care if anyone else is listening or not."

Gage shrugged. "That's not a way to get love and respect, either."

Definitely no smile this time. Ford's eyes narrowed. "You're just like your grandfather. He was cocky, too."

Gage hadn't intended to go there tonight, but he would now that Ford had opened the door. "Did you even have any proof he was sleeping with your wife?"

"Oh, yes. I followed her to his place. The place you later used to bed Lynette. The shame of the mother passed down to the daughter."

It turned Gage's stomach to hear this man's venom, especially when the venom was directed at Lynette. And at his grandfather.

"Did you kill him, too?" Gage came right out and asked.

Now, Ford smiled. "Wouldn't you love to know? Oh, and just so we're on the same page. If you're still alive when this conversation is over, you won't be leaving until my men have searched *you* for a wire. I like to keep my secrets safe within my own family."

Gage didn't intend to let Ford or one of his goon-guards lay a hand on him.

"So, I think what we have here is a stalemate," Ford continued. "You're not leaving with Lynette, and I'm not stopping until I find out what she learned from snooping in my private files."

"Yeah, you're right, we do have a stalemate." And that's all Gage said for several seconds. Ford's guards were already looking antsy, and a good, long pause would only add to it. "Well, maybe not. After all, I'm a better shot than either of those Neanderthals."

"I thought you didn't want to kill me."

"No. I do." Another pause. "It's just when your men get nervous enough—and they will—they'll fire. You'll pull your weapon, too. It's a reflex. Anyone armed would, and I know you're armed with a slide holster. Ankle, too." Gage took a step closer, lowered his voice to a whisper. "And when you pull is when you'll die."

And the staring match began.

Gage wasn't bluffing, so that helped. But he wasn't

sure how much longer it would take to make those two start firing.

The walkie-talkie made a soft buzzing sound, and without taking his eyes off Ford, Gage used his left hand to click it on.

"We got trouble," Mason said. Before Gage could even manage a word, his brother added, "It's Lynette. She just pulled up in a cruiser and parked in front of the courthouse steps."

Gage cursed.

Ford smiled.

"Lynette's not alone," Mason added. "Nate, Dade and Kade are with her."

That was good. Except there was something in Mason's voice that said otherwise. And there was definitely something up with Ford.

Why the devil had Lynette risked everything to come here?

Gage was sure he wouldn't like the answer.

"Lynette and the others aren't our only visitors," Mason explained. "Dalvetti and his men rammed through the road barriers I put up, and they just arrived, too."

There wasn't enough profanity in Gage's vocabulary to cover what he felt. Lynette was here. Why, he didn't know, but he did know she was in grave danger.

"Cover Lynette," Gage insisted, already heading for the door while he kept watch on the three vipers inside.

Gage pointed his gun at the two guards. "On the floor, hands behind your head."

They looked at Ford, and Gage held his breath. He didn't have time for this, and if they didn't do as he ordered, he'd have to neutralize them. Maybe a shot or two to the kneecaps. Yeah, he'd have to answer for it later, but it would give him a fighting chance at saving Lynette.

Ford gave his men a nod. Just that simple gesture. And the two lowered themselves to the floor. It was probably some kind of trap, a move they'd planned, but Gage had to deal with Lynette first.

Gage had barely taken a step when he heard something else that he hadn't wanted to hear.

A blast. Outside.

Right where the cruiser was parked.

Chapter Seventeen

The second that Kade brought the cruiser to a stop in front of the courthouse, Lynette tried to bolt. She had her gun drawn and ready, and she had to get to Gage *now*.

But Nate clamped his hand on her arm to stop her.

Good thing, too.

Because Lynette hadn't even gotten the door open when there was an explosion.

Her heart jumped to her throat.

Chunks of concrete and asphalt slammed into the cruiser, shaking it like an earthquake. One of those chunks flew into the front end and gashed the metal hood directly into the engine.

"I think someone just used a rocket launcher on us," Kade spit out. "Thank God they missed."

Yes, thank God. But it'd still done a lot of damage.

She couldn't see who'd fired it and didn't have time to look around. Dade dragged her into the backseat with him. He shoved her onto the floor and covered her body with his.

She heard Nate and Kade scrambling around in the front seat, and it was only a few seconds before Mason's voice poured through Kade's walkie-talkie.

"It's Dalvetti and his men. Three of them, all hiding behind the new hotel," Mason added. Each word was punctuated with a burst of his heavy breath. "I just took out the guy with the launcher, and none of the others has one."

Oh, mercy. Lynette was thankful Mason had managed to do that much. But it meant killers were still out there, and while they might not have another rocket launcher, they almost certainly had guns.

"Any of you hurt?" Mason asked.

Lynette did a quick inventory. The cruiser was damaged beyond repair, and they'd been darn lucky that the blast hadn't landed on them. She was certain all of Gage's brothers were thinking *I told you so,* but Lynette didn't regret her decision.

Not yet anyway.

"Where's Gage?" she shouted to Mason.

"Inside." Mason paused a heartbeat. "With your father and his two bodyguards."

Not bodyguards. Goons. Goons who would try to kill him if her father didn't do the job first.

"I've lost contact with Gage," Mason added a moment later.

He couldn't have said anything else that would have put that much terror in her. Sweet heaven. Were they holding Gage at gunpoint? Or had they already hurt him? She refused to even consider that it might be worse than that.

"Gage can handle himself," Mason reminded her.

Maybe, but he was outnumbered and therefore outgunned. Now, here they were pinned down, and they had to get to him so they could help.

"Where are Dalvetti and these gunmen?" Kade asked Mason. But the question had no sooner left his mouth when someone fired again.

This one slammed right into the driver's side of the cruiser. Whoever was shooting, the Rylands and she were clearly the target. And worse, the cruiser was disabled. There was no way Kade could drive them out of there.

The next bullet had a different sound and angle, and it took her a moment to realize it'd come from the roof of the courthouse.

"I got another one of them," Mason let them know. "Not Dalvetti himself though. He's staying back."

More shots, and this time they didn't come at the cruiser. There was a gunfight going down on Main Street, just yards from sleepy little shops.

"Is Lynette okay?" she heard someone ask.

Gage.

It was his voice now on the walkie-talkie.

"I'm fine. Are you all right?" Lynette couldn't ask Gage fast enough.

"Mad as the devil for you coming here." But his voice softened. "Yeah, I'm okay. Just trying to take out Dalvetti's men while playing stalemate with your father."

Lynette didn't like the sound of that. Or the next round of bullets. The shooters were hitting the cruiser again. One of the bullets gouged into the already damaged windshield.

"To heck with this," Kade snarled. "We have to get Lynette out of here."

More bullets came at them, nonstop now, but she could also hear Mason and the others on the rooftop returning fire. As Dade pinned her down on the floorboard, she was able to catch a glimpse of Gage.

Alive and unharmed.

He stepped out from the courthouse doorway and fired in Dalvetti's direction.

"Is it safe to get Lynette and the rest of us in there?" Kade asked.

"No. But from the looks of things out there, we don't have a choice. Get her in as fast as you can."

Kade did move fast. So did Dade. He pushed her to the side of the cruiser that was facing the courthouse doors. She was already wearing a Kevlar vest that Dade had given her before they left the sheriff's office, but as Gage had pointed out, that wouldn't help with a head shot.

"We're moving now," Dade told his brothers.

Lynette didn't know what Nate and Kade would do with that information, but they knew. While Dade got her out of the cruiser, both Nate and Kade started firing at Dalvetti and what was left of his hit squad.

Dade and she barreled up the three steps, and she got a closer look at Gage. She felt both the overwhelming relief in one breath, and in the next, she felt the overwhelming fear. With the bullets flying, they might not be *alive and unharmed* for long.

Gage didn't look directly at her. He kept his attention fastened to the shooters by her office. He took aim. And fired.

Three thick blasts.

She heard someone groan in pain, and from the corner of her eye, Lynette saw one of Dalvetti's gunmen fall to the ground.

When she made it to him, Gage latched on to her and pulled her inside. Dade was right behind them, but he stayed in the doorway and started delivering some shots of his own at Dalvetti.

"Why did you come?" Gage demanded. *"Why?"*

She shook her head and hated the worry and fear in his voice. "I didn't have a choice. My father called and made a veiled threat that if I didn't come, he'd kill you."

Gage took aim at the men on the floor. But then he glanced around the lobby and cursed. "He got away."

Because the thoughts and fear were flying through her head, it took her a moment to realize what Gage meant. She looked around, as well, and didn't see the one person responsible for all of his.

Her father was gone.

HELL. THIS WAS NOT the way Gage wanted all of this to play out.

All he'd wanted was to negotiate some kind of truce with Ford and then leave so he could take Lynette far away from Silver Creek. That way, all of them would have walked out alive.

But now, things had gotten complicated in a dangerous way.

Because Lynette was here.

And her father wasn't.

"Get down," Gage told Lynette, and he pointed to the staircase banister.

Gage was betting Ford hadn't used the stairs to escape since the stairs were right by the door where Gage had been standing. And shooting.

If *escape* was what Ford had actually done.

It was possible the man was lurking in that dark hall and was ready to strike. After all, there had to be a reason Ford had told Lynette to come here. Later, Gage would figure out what that reason was, and he was pretty sure he wasn't going to like it.

"Disarm these two," Gage told Dade. "And cuff them if you can."

The walkie-talkie buzzed again, and Gage hit the button while he inched his way toward the hall.

"The only one left outside is Dalvetti," Mason relayed. "I took out his other man. That's the good news. The bad news is that he's in a Hummer, and he's driving straight toward the courthouse. I think he's planning to drive up the steps and bash it through the front door."

Well, Gage hadn't thought this could get worse, but he'd obviously been wrong.

Gage looked out the front glass door where Nate and Kade were shooting at a massive black Hummer that was flying across the parking lot. The windows in the vehicle must have been bulletproof, because no shots seemed to be getting through.

They had seconds at most to get out of the path of that vehicle.

"Move!" Gage told Dade, who was still in the process of disarming Ford's henchmen.

Gage grabbed Lynette and started running. Yeah, it was a risk to use either the stairs or head to the hall, but at the moment the biggest risk of all was staying put. He started up the stairs with her.

Dade left the men and hurried to the back of the foyer by the hall. Neither of Ford's men stayed put, and Gage couldn't blame them. They scrambled out of the way.

"Watch out for Ford," Gage called down to warn his brother.

But he wasn't sure Dade heard him because at the exact moment Gage shouted that warning, Dalvetti's Hummer tore up the steps and came crashing through the doors.

Glass and wood flew everywhere, like missiles shooting in every direction. Even though Lynette and he were only halfway up the stairs, Gage stopped, shoved her behind him so that she wouldn't get hit with the flying debris, and he got ready to fire. So did Dade.

But not for long.

One of Ford's gunmen must have figured out this was a good time to make a bad situation worse because he drew a gun from the waist of his pants and took aim at

Dade. His brother dived into the hall just in the nick of time, and he came up ready to return fire.

The gunman's shot slammed into the wall, and he scrambled for cover, as well, on the side of a table stacked with pamphlets.

Behind him, Gage felt Lynette move and realized she, too, was taking aim at the second henchman who'd drawn his weapon. She fired, the blast roaring through Gage's head.

She missed.

And Gage volleyed his attention between Ford's men and Dalvetti's car. The windows were heavily tinted so he couldn't see the drug lord inside, but Gage had no doubt he was there. Ditto for his brothers outside. Nate, Kade and Mason would soon be coming in to help. The trick would be to make sure that none of them got killed in the process.

Especially Lynette.

When she took another shot at her father's men, Gage pushed her back down. He appreciated the help, but he didn't want her to be an easy target, not when shots could come from so many different directions.

"Stay down and watch behind us," he told her. Just in case he'd been wrong about Ford not using the stairs. He didn't want her father or anybody else sneaking up on them for an easy ambush.

There was another shot in Dade's direction, but Gage couldn't look to see what'd happened. That's because the door to the Hummer eased open just a fraction, a rifle barrel jutted out, and a bullet came zinging their way. It slammed into the wall behind them.

Gage sent a shot directly at the rifle.

He'd been right about the bulletproof part. His shot

collided into the glass, but it didn't penetrate. That meant he had to draw Dalvetti out of the vehicle.

Dalvetti fired again, and Gage had no choice but to get down as well. He tried to use his body to shield Lynette, but there was always a possibility that a bullet could go through him and hit her.

And the baby.

That sickened and riled him. This was the last thing he'd wanted for Lynette and the child.

Behind the Hummer, Gage could see Nate and Kade making their way up the steps. Both had their weapons drawn, and that meant Dalvetti was trapped.

Or maybe not.

The man fired off two more shots with his rifle, and Gage heard him hit the accelerator. Dalvetti was about to attempt an escape, and he just might get away with it. That couldn't happen. It would only give him a chance to regroup and come back again for another attack.

"Get out of the way!" Gage shouted to Nate and Kade.

They did. His brothers dived to the side just as the Hummer jolted backward.

Gage kept his gun aimed and was ready to race down the stairs after him, but the edge of the Hummer's door caught on to what was left of the courthouse entrance. The door flew open.

And Gage saw Dalvetti behind the wheel.

The look that passed between them only lasted a split second, but it was enough for Gage to see the awareness of his situation register in the man's murderous eyes.

Awareness and something else he didn't have the time to figure out.

Gage pulled the trigger.

Not once. But twice. And he sent two shots directly into Dalvetti's head.

It was never easy to kill a man, *never,* but Gage couldn't regret this one. Dalvetti would have murdered them all if Gage hadn't ended this now.

Except it hadn't ended.

Dalvetti hadn't been the only killer in the building. Gage swung in Dade's direction just as one of Ford's henchmen took aim again at his brother. Gage aimed, too, but the shots came from the front of the building.

From Kade and Nate.

Each of them took out Ford's men.

"We have to get out of here," Gage immediately told Lynette. Because while three men were dead, the most dangerous one of the lot was still missing. Plus, there was the possibility that Ford wasn't alone. Either Nicole or Patrick could be inside or nearby waiting to help Ford out.

Gage would have to postpone that fight.

After he had Lynette far away from this place.

"We can use the Hummer," Gage instructed.

He took Lynette's hand and got her moving down the stairs. That way, if Ford or someone else did start shooting, the bullets wouldn't be able to get to Lynette. Of course, that meant pulling Dalvetti's body out of the vehicle first, and it wouldn't be a pleasant task with Lynette right there to watch. Gage wished there were another way because Lynette had already seen enough death for one night.

Kade hurried to the driver's side of the Hummer, and he looked in. His brother cursed. "Get away from the vehicle!" he shouted. "Now!"

Gage didn't ask why, and neither did his other brothers. All of them started to run.

Nate and Kade raced back outside and Dade ran deeper

into the hall. Gage headed back upstairs with Lynette and braced himself for whatever the hell was about to happen.

Behind them, the Hummer burst into flames.

Chapter Eighteen

Lynette caught just a glimpse of the fire before Gage put her back down on the steps and flattened himself over her.

"Dalvetti rigged the fire," she heard Gage say.

So, that's why it had simply burst into flames. Maybe the man had done that to destroy evidence. Or considering it was Dalvetti's vehicle, maybe it was meant to kill them. A way to reach out from beyond death and make sure they all died with him.

If they'd gotten inside, it might have done just that.

"The gas tank could explode," Gage told her.

Lynette hadn't exactly started to breathe easier, but she had thought for a moment that at least one threat was gone.

Apparently not.

Gage caught on to her again, pulling her to her feet, and they raced up the remainder of the steps together. She had just a glimpse of Nate and Kade, both outside, and both were hurrying across the parking lot and away from the Hummer time bomb. She couldn't see Dade, but she prayed he was doing the same.

When they reached the top, Gage slowed and looked around. First at the long stretch of offices just behind the balcony to their right and then at the equally long corridor on their left. Both were pitch-black, and he pushed up the light switch on the wall.

Nothing happened.

Lynette wanted to curse. "Someone's cut the power," she whispered.

Maybe Dalvetti or one of his men was responsible. Maybe her father. But she doubted it was a power outage. No. Someone had done this to give him or her an advantage for either escape or attack.

She figured with their luck, it was the latter.

"We have to find a way out," Gage insisted. "Keep watch behind us."

She managed a nod. Managed to make brief eye contact with him, too. Gage was focused on the situation, on getting them out of there, but he took a second to brush a kiss on her cheek. Then, he was all cowboy secret agent again.

Behind them, at the bottom of the stairs, there was a thick blast, a lot louder than the one that'd disabled the cruiser. It rumbled through the building, shaking every inch of it.

Oh, mercy.

Lynette had braced herself for the gas tank to explode, but she'd had no idea that it would be that loud. Framed pictures tumbled from the walls and crashed to the floor, and bits of the acoustic ceiling hailed down on them. But the walls held.

Thank God.

Now, she only hoped that Gage's brothers had gotten far enough away from the blast so they weren't injured. She hated every moment of this. The fear. The worry. The realization that Gage and his brothers could die because of her. Because of her father.

"There's a fire escape at the back of the building," she let Gage know.

Basically, it was a metal landing with stairs leading down to the ground. Maybe Ford hadn't managed to block it somehow. Also maybe the fire department was already on the way because she was certain that by now someone had called them. Especially since the gas tank explosion had no doubt started a fire.

The back of the building wasn't really that far. Only about sixty feet. But between the fire escape and them were offices.

Lots of them.

Plenty of places for someone to hide.

Lynette prayed that all of Dalvetti's men were gone or dead, and she added to her prayer that her father had retreated, as well. Of course, that left Patrick or Nicole. Her father could have told one or both about this meeting. In fact, he could have arranged the get-together so that either Patrick or Nicole would be the triggerman to kill Gage.

That way, her father could get someone else to do his dirty work.

The anger slammed through her, along with the fear that they were still in danger. Always would be. As long as her father drew breath. Because even though he'd failed tonight didn't mean there wouldn't be another episode.

When the black smoke began to coil its way up the stairs, Gage and she picked up the pace and started down the hall. Lynette put her back to Gage and kept her gun ready. Even though she'd missed the henchman when she'd fired, she tried to keep her hand steady. Tried to be ready for anything.

They passed the first office. The door was closed, and she checked to make sure it was locked.

It was.

Of course, someone could have locked it from inside, but at least she might be able to hear the person when or if they tried to open the door and attack.

She repeated the process with the next office. And the next. Until they'd made it nearly halfway down the hall.

The sound stopped both Gage and her.

She lifted her head, listening.

Was it the crackling noise from the fire? Yet something else falling from the blast?

Or was it something worse?

There were a lot of things that could fit into that *something worse* category.

"See anything?" Gage whispered.

Lynette looked around, but it was too dark to see much. There was smoke, thready streams near the stairs, but she didn't see anything else. However, she did hear something.

Sirens.

The fire department was on the way, though they might not just go bursting into the building until they'd assessed the situation. It was also possible they couldn't get in the building and might have to try to extinguish the fire from outside.

"Let's go," Gage insisted, and he started to move again.

An icy chill went through her, and even though she hadn't seen anything, Lynette sensed that something was wrong.

She heard the soft click on her left and pivoted in that direction.

But it was already too late.

Someone threw open one of those office doors and knocked the weapon from her hand. It clattered onto the floor.

And before she could retrieve it, there was someone pointing a gun right at her.

GAGE DIDN'T MISS the small gasp that Lynette made.

He turned just in time to see her gun go flying. He also saw the person who'd caused the gasp and the fallen gun.

Ford.

But while Lynette was no longer armed, her father sure was. And he had his firearm aimed at Lynette. And not just *at* her. Toward her stomach.

Hell.

This was about to get ugly fast. Especially since his brothers were no doubt trying to make their way to Lynette and him. There were a lot of possibilities for mistakes, distractions and especially bullets.

"Drop your gun," Gage warned the man, and he went closer, even though he knew he didn't have much bargaining power with that gun pointed at Lynette.

"You move another foot, and there'll be no more baby," Ford warned right back.

Lynette shook her head, motioning for Gage to stop. He did. But he couldn't stop the rage at this monster threatening an unborn child.

It took a special piece of slime to do that.

"I guess this means no more stalemate," Ford said with victory in his voice. "Well, there won't be after you drop your weapons. And you will drop them. Put them on the floor and slide them against the wall."

Gage debated it. He hated to surrender both of his guns, but he couldn't risk Ford shooting Lynette. Of course, once Gage was unarmed, he would try to shoot her anyway.

Well, maybe.

Lynette lowered her hand to her pocket. Ford reacted. Man, did he. He shoved the gun closer to her.

"You said put down the weapons," Lynette clarified. She fished around in her pocket and came out with a small police-issue handgun. No doubt something one of his brothers had given her. She eased it onto the floor and kicked it away from her.

Too bad she hadn't held on to it.

Because they might need it before this was over.

Whatever *this* was.

Outside, he heard the fire engines screech to a stop. Good. They'd put out that fire, but it would be a while—too long—before they could climb up those stairs. That meant Gage had to buy them some time.

"What's this all about?" Gage demanded, looking straight at Ford. "Are you working with Patrick or Nicole?"

Ford made a mock huffing sound. "No. Neither of them knows anything about this. They were just convenient tools. Or so I thought. I told them Lynette had found something incriminating, but sadly they didn't do anything about it except make threats and get angry."

"You thought you'd incite one of them to kill me," Lynette said. Her voice was surprisingly strong, and there was rage in it.

Not good.

Rage usually meant a person was willing to do something risky. Gage didn't want her taking any more risks.

"I thought Patrick and Nicole would *scare* you," Ford corrected. "So that you'd come to me for help."

"To you for help?" Lynette questioned. "And why would I do that?"

"I was your last resort. Well, after Gage. But I'd planned on Dalvetti getting him out of the picture tonight. You just can't get good help these days, not even when they're so-called bloodthirsty drug lords out for revenge. That idiot made a mess of things downstairs."

Gage had to fight back rage, too. How dare this SOB

act so cavalierly about something so deadly. He wished he could beat Ford to a pulp. And he just might before this was over.

"Your guns," Ford reminded Gage. "Put them on the floor now."

Gage laid down his primary and kicked it in the direction of Lynette's gun, but he took his time taking out the weapon from his slide holster in the back of his jeans. What he needed was a way out of this, and he wanted to hang on to his weapon as long as possible to make that happen.

"Are you saying you had no plans to kill Lynette?" Gage asked. Yeah, it was a distraction question, but he really did want to know what was going on inside that sick mind.

"No plans for that," Ford assured him. "Still don't have any. The hit man was just supposed to fire shots at her, that's all."

"He didn't listen," Gage said through clenched teeth. "He fired into her dark bedroom."

Ford shrugged. "Disappointing, yes. But you took care of him for me. And Lynette. I appreciate that."

"Thanks," Gage growled. But he damn sure hadn't saved Lynette so he could hand her over to Ford like this. "What happens now? How are you *not* going to kill Lynette this time?"

"Easy. When we're done here, she'll go back to the mental institution in Mexico for some experimental drug therapy. I've heard it does wonders for personality adjustment…and some memory loss. In a few months she might be ready for a return trip home."

Gage nearly broke his fingers with the hard grip he had on his backup weapon. He judged the angle, hoping he had a shot, but he didn't. Ford had moved so that Lynette was essentially his human shield.

"You're going to brainwash me," Lynette concluded.

Ford lifted his shoulder. "I suppose you could call it that."

Yeah, it would be exactly that. God knows what those drugs would do to Lynette's mind and the baby. Plus, Lynette wasn't just going to submit. She'd fight back.

And lose.

Downstairs, Gage could hear the firemen entering the building. If that made Ford nervous, he darn sure didn't show it. The man was cool and unruffled.

"The stairs are impassable," Ford remarked. "Don't count on your firemen friends or your brothers to get up here to help you out."

Oh, but they would.

But Gage rethought that when he studied the hallway and Ford made a sound deep within his throat. It sounded smug, or something.

"What did you do?" Gage demanded.

"I blocked the fire escape. No one's coming in that way any time soon."

Gage didn't bother cursing out loud, but that was not good news. Still, his brothers were resourceful, and they'd figure out a way to get in eventually. Gage got busy with some time-buying.

"We're really supposed to believe you don't want Lynette dead?" Gage asked.

"A shot to my stomach could kill me," Lynette pointed out.

Oh, man. She was shaking all over now, including her voice, and not from fear, either. If Gage didn't do something soon, she was going to launch herself right at her father.

"Then don't take the risk," Ford warned her. He used the barrel of his weapon to motion at Gage again. "Your gun, on the floor. If I have to repeat it again, Agent Ryland, I will pull this trigger."

Gage didn't doubt it. And that meant he had just one shot at this. He would lean down. To the side. So that Lynette was no longer in his line of fire. Gage would pretend to put the gun on the floor.

Then, he could yell for Lynette to get down.

And Gage would fire.

The plan sucked, and there were so many things that could go wrong. Too many. But their odds weren't so hot with Ford calling the shots, either.

"Can I say goodbye to Lynette?" Gage asked the man. It would be a fake goodbye, but he wanted to say it anyway. Every word might buy them some time, because he might be able to distract Ford.

Or goad him into doing something he hadn't planned—like aiming that gun at Gage instead of Lynette.

If that happened, Ford was a dead man.

Ford hesitated. "Make your goodbye quick."

Lynette's back was to him, but she looked over her shoulder at him.

"I'm glad I had you in my bed tonight," Gage said. Words meant to set Ford's teeth on edge. "It was like old times."

Lynette smiled. A forced one. But hey, if Ford could see it, it would still get to dear ol' dad. "Gage, you're the only man I've ever loved."

Okay.

That didn't sound like words for Ford. But for Gage.

Years ago, she'd told him that she loved him. Too many times to count. But that was *years ago*. Before they'd broken each other's heart and gone their separate ways. Before her father had ripped them apart.

Something he was still trying his damnedest to do.

Lynette's fake smile faded, and even though he couldn't see them, Gage thought there might be tears in her eyes. "And I'll love you and this baby until the day I die."

Ford made a sound of utter disgust.

Gage still had hold of his gun, but he wasn't in position to fire because Lynette was in front of her father.

But time had run out.

The risk of staying put was far greater than the risk of doing what he had to do. Gage pushed Lynette out of the way and came up ready to fire. He did.

So did Ford.

Both shots blasted through the air.

Chapter Nineteen

Lynette shouted for her father to stop. But she knew it wouldn't do any good.

He fired at Gage anyway.

It missed, thank God.

The shot slammed into the wall next to Gage.

But her father immediately ducked into the dark office, and he reaimed. Fired.

She watched the whole nightmare unfold. In slow motion. As she tumbled to the floor. Helpless to do anything to stop another bullet from slamming into Gage.

And it did.

The bullet tore through Gage's right arm.

Lynette landed hard on her shoulder, out of harm's way. But not Gage. He was in the worst place possible—out in the open and in a direct line of fire. Her father was ready to pull the trigger again.

And she couldn't let that happen.

Heaven knows how badly Gage was already hurt, and she couldn't risk another shot.

She kicked at her father and barely made contact with his shin. It was just enough to distract him. He looked down. Her father aimed the gun.

At her.

Gage made a feral sound, and despite his gunshot

wound, he dived right at Ford. They collided and went flying back deeper into the office.

Lynette didn't know if her father had managed to hang on to his gun, but if he had, it was only a matter of time before he'd fire it again. She scurried across the floor and retrieved the handgun that Dade had given her before they left the sheriff's office.

She took aim.

But couldn't shoot.

The darkness was only part of the problem. Her father and Gage were in a fight for their lives, their bodies tangled around each other, and it would be impossible to fire and not risk hitting Gage.

She saw Gage's fist slam against her father's face. But she also saw something else.

The gun in her father's hand.

Her heart sank. Because his finger was still on the trigger.

She wanted to shout to Gage to be careful, but at this point, her warning would only be an unnecessary distraction. Lynette tried to remind herself that he was a trained federal agent. He'd no doubt been in situations like this. But he was hurt and unarmed.

He needed her help.

Lynette inched forward, waiting and looking for any chance to kick her father or even shoot. The chance didn't come. Ford angled the gun.

Fired again.

And Lynette watched in horror as the bullet slammed into Gage's chest. He flew back, gasping for air.

Maybe dying.

He couldn't die. He just couldn't.

The tears burned her eyes. The fear had her by the

throat. But she forced herself to move. She didn't know how because everything was on autopilot now.

Ford lifted the gun, took aim at Gage again, but Lynette shouted, "No!"

Her father looked at her, just a split second, and she kicked at the gun. To her surprise, he stopped. Well, for just that second. And then he whipped out another gun from his pocket.

He aimed one gun at her.

And one at Gage.

She glanced at Gage. He was still gasping. And he ripped open his shirt so she could see the Kevlar vest. Like the one she was wearing.

The relief flooded through her.

He wasn't dead. He hadn't been shot in the chest. But he was injured, and she had no idea how badly. She only knew she had to get him to the hospital. Hopefully, there was already an ambulance on the way. But she seriously doubted that her father planned to let Gage get the help he needed.

"Put down that gun," Ford ordered her.

"No." And Lynette didn't hesitate.

Her father made a sound of amusement. "I killed the last woman who told me that."

"My mother?" Though she already knew the answer.

"Your mother," he verified, volleying glances between Gage and her. Gage was doing the same while fighting for air and clutching his chest. He was also inching his hand toward his gun that had fallen on the floor.

"You drowned her because she said no to you?" Lynette asked, and she didn't bother to tone down the hatred. She wanted her father's full attention on her so that Gage could get that gun.

"Of course. She was a tramp, you know. She refused to

stop seeing her lover." He laughed. It was hollow and cold. "You should have seen her face when I told her that Sheriff Chet McLaurin was dead. She fell apart, dropped down on her knees, sobbing. Killing her was easy after that."

Every detail turned her stomach and made her want to pull the trigger. But she couldn't risk that, not while her father still had that weapon aimed at Gage.

From the corner of her eye, she saw Gage ease his hand over the gun.

"That's what will happen to you when I kill Gage," Ford warned. "You'll fall apart. You'll need the asylum after that."

Lynette shook her head. "I'm not letting you kill Gage. I didn't stand up to you ten years ago, but I'm doing it now."

He laughed again. "You can't shoot me. You're not a killer, Lynette."

No. She wasn't. But she would do whatever was necessary to protect the man she loved.

She waited until Gage had the gun in his hand before she asked her father a final question. "You think you'll get away with murder again?" she pushed.

"Of course. I'm a man of money and resources. With Gage dead, and you committed to the asylum, there'll be no witnesses. No one to tell the story of what happened here tonight."

She looked him straight in the eyes. "Don't be so sure of that." Lynette paused. "I have a tape recorder in my pocket, and I turned it on when I took out the handgun. I've got your confession to two murders and the attempted murder of a federal agent."

Because she was staring at him, she saw her father's eyes widen. Heard the jolt of breath. He opened his mouth, probably to say she was lying.

She wasn't.

And her expression must have let him know that.

Lynette heard the footsteps in the hall. Someone was running toward them. The Rylands, no doubt. They'd finally made it through the barricade on the fire escape.

"Soon, this room will be filled with lawmen, and one of them will cuff you. Read your rights. And haul you off to jail." She kept her attention nailed to her father. "I'll be there when you're convicted of murder. When you're disgraced and the talk of every gossip in the state."

Gage shook his head. "Stay back, Lynette." She did, but she didn't stop staring at her father. "And I'll also be there when they shove a needle into your arm." Her chin came up. "I got you, you bastard."

Ford moved so fast that even though she was tuned in to his every move, she still didn't see it coming. His hand flexed. Ready to pull the trigger.

But he didn't shoot at her. Or Gage.

Senator Ford Herrington turned the gun on himself. And fired.

Chapter Twenty

Gage felt as if he'd been kicked in the chest by an ornery rodeo bull. His arm where he'd been shot wasn't feeling too good, either. But he was alive and nearly in one piece. And the best part?

Lynette didn't have a scratch on her.

How she'd come out of that nightmare unscathed was nothing short of a miracle, but it was a miracle that Gage would take. But he rethought that. No injuries, but she looked on the verge of losing it as Mason and Kade helped Gage into the emergency room. Nate and Dade were right behind them.

"He's been shot," Lynette called out to the entire E.R.

And the place wasn't exactly empty. Grayson and his brothers' wives were all there: Darcy, Kayla and Bree. The kids, too. Three of them, Robbie, Noah and Kimmie, were toddling around while Darcy and Kayla held twin baby girls who looked to be a couple of months old. Kade and Bree's, no doubt.

"Are we having a family reunion?" Gage asked.

But his joke went over like a lead balloon because the women turned pasty-white, and Darcy immediately motioned for a medic.

"He needs help *now*," Lynette insisted.

Actually, he didn't, but Gage figured that wasn't an

argument he was going to win when it came to the *now* part. The bleeding had stopped. He could breathe without writhing in pain. And he was more than a little pleased that Lynette and his baby were no longer in danger. A bit of pain and blood were a small price to pay for that.

"This way," a medic said, hurrying toward them. He grabbed a wheelchair, put Gage in it, and without stopping, he wheeled him into the examining room.

"You can wait outside," the medic said when Lynette followed.

"No. I can't," she insisted right back.

Most of the others came, too, all of them peering at Gage and his injuries. Only Kayla stayed back with the three toddlers, probably because she didn't want them to see the blood on Gage's arm.

Gage didn't want them to see that, either.

He hadn't been able to shield his family from the danger, but there was no reason to add to the trauma that'd just happened.

"How badly are you hurt?" Darcy asked, handing the baby girl to Kade.

Gage was about to say *"not bad,"* but Lynette answered for him. "He has a gunshot wound to the arm. He's wearing Kevlar, but he took a direct shot to the chest."

All the lawmen and Bree winced. Probably because they knew how it felt.

"Yeah, it hurts all right," Gage complained but then hated that it only caused Lynette to look even more concerned. Soon, he would have to do something to get that concerned, pained look off her face.

He'd have to do some fence-mending with his family, too.

Gage glanced at each member of his Ryland clan. Even

with the pain, it was good to be here. Even better to be surrounded by blood who had his back.

"You a dad yet?" Gage asked Grayson while the medic started easing off Gage's shirt.

"I am." Grayson smiled from ear to ear. "A boy. Eight pounds, nine ounces."

"He's a big one," Darcy added. "But Eve's doing great. We were with them when we got Dade's call that you were coming in to the E.R."

"The baby's a Ryland through and through," Grayson went on. "Dark hair. Our gray eyes. Built like a cowboy. We've named him Chet David."

After their grandfather. It was a good legacy to continue. It was also reminder that in about seven and a half months, Lynette and he would have their own little cowboy or cowgirl. Gender didn't matter to him. Gage was just thankful this baby could have a safe, normal life. Especially after the unsafe, nonnormal start.

Gage looked at Lynette again to see how she was dealing with all of this and her father's death, but she had her attention fastened on him.

"I'm so sorry I couldn't stop this from happening," she whispered.

He caught on to her hand, even though the movement hurt, and he eased her closer. "You stopped it just fine. Later though, I'll be riled at you for going to the courthouse in the first place."

Riled, for at least five seconds.

Gage pulled her down for a kiss that was probably too long and too hot considering they had an audience.

"Told you they were back together," Mason mumbled.

"I don't think they were ever apart," Kade corrected. "Never could keep their hands off each other."

Gage was amused at this speculation about his personal

life, but not so amused that Lynette still looked ready to drop. He had her sit on the edge of the examining table while the medic kept on working, kept on clearing away the blood on his wound.

"We left Mel and Luis at the courthouse," Dade relayed to Grayson.

The other deputies, Gage recalled. He felt sorry for them. Working that crime scene was going to be a bear. Dead bodies always were.

"I'll go back in a few minutes and check on things," Dade added. "It won't be long before the press gets wind of this."

Dade was right. A senator's suicide would make the front page for a while. Maybe he could talk Lynette into staying away from a newspaper and a television for the next couple of weeks. Even her own newspaper. He didn't want her reliving that even if he couldn't completely shield her from the necessary follow-up that Grayson would have to do.

"I have something for your investigation," Lynette volunteered. She reached in her pocket, took out the tape recorder and handed it to Grayson.

So, it hadn't been a bluff after all. She had finally gotten the evidence to prove that her father was a cold-blooded killer. And a coward, of course.

"My father made a confession of sorts before he killed himself," Lynette added. She looked back at Gage.

And he finished for her. "Ford murdered Lynette's mother and Granddaddy Chet."

The silence slipped through the room, and even the young medic stopped and volleyed glances at all of them. There probably wasn't a person in Silver Creek who hadn't heard of their grandfather's murder, the way he'd been gunned down by an unknown assailant.

The gossip had never stopped.

Neither had the family's pain.

Some folks had even whispered that Gage's father, Boone, had been the one to pull the trigger. Or maybe Gage's mother. Perhaps Lynette's mother, too, since there had also been gossip about the affair between Chet and her. But Ford's reputation hadn't made him a top-list suspect. Well, except in Gage's and Lynette's minds.

Later, each of his brothers would have to deal with the loss in their own way.

But it wasn't a wound that would completely heal.

Ever.

Gage didn't have any training in psychology, but it didn't take a shrink to know they were all in law enforcement because of their grandfather. Chet McLaurin had made them all the men they were today.

And his murder had sealed their fates.

Gage mentally shrugged. There were much worse fates and paths that could have been sealed. At least they were all on the good side of the law.

Mason's favorite saying was right. *Justice isn't just coming—it's already here.*

"I can take over," Gage heard someone say, the voice cutting through the silence.

Dr. Mickelson shoved back the green curtain and stepped around the others. Gage had known the lanky doc his entire life. Heck, the man had delivered him, but apparently he was still going strong.

"Welcome home, Gage," the doctor greeted. "You Ryland boys are keeping me in business with these gunshot wounds. And babies." He gave one of the twin's toes a playful jiggle. "I don't guess it'd do any good to ask y'all to go in the waiting room?"

No one budged.

"Didn't think so." The doctor flexed his eyebrows. "Well, if you're squeamish or prone to puking, look away, because a gunshot wound isn't pretty."

Dr. Mickelson peeled off the rest of Gage's shirt, and Lynette went pale again.

"It's not that bad, Lynette," the doctor assured her, even though he hadn't done more than glance at her. The doctor had delivered her, too. "Looks like the bullet went through and through."

The medic unstrapped the Kevlar vest, and Gage saw the makings of an ugly bruise near the center of his chest. Ford might have been a coward, but he was clearly a good shot. If Gage hadn't been wearing the vest, the bullet would have gone through his heart.

"You'll need that wound dressed," the doctor continued. "And a chest X-ray to make sure your ribs aren't cracked. Your family and Lynette can't be there for that."

"Lynette is my family," Gage corrected. "She's my wife."

The doc flexed his eyebrows again, made a sound of approval and turned to her. "We'll get Gage all stitched up and then check you out, too. You're looking a little peaked there."

"I'm pregnant," she confessed, never taking her attention off Gage.

Dr. Mickelson made another sound of approval. Darcy and Nate made a sound of a different kind. Surprised ones.

"When are you due?" Nate asked.

"Early May," Lynette answered.

"Me, too," Darcy said, explaining the reason for the surprised sounds.

Mason just groaned. "None of you better expect me

to change diapers. Or babysit." He took the tape recorder from Grayson. "I'll get started on the paperwork."

Mason gave Lynette and him a glance that Gage decided to interpret as brotherly affection. Coming from Mason, it was practically warm and fuzzy.

The others weren't so subtle. They came forward in a wave to hug Lynette and offer congrats and good wishes. It wasn't quiet, but the doctor tolerated it for several moments before he hitched his thumb to the waiting room.

"The sooner I do this, the sooner you can take him home," Dr. Mickelson said.

That sent them all scattering. All but Lynette. And she still had that terrified look in her eyes. Gage decided this couldn't wait for X-rays and stitches.

"Could you give us a minute?" he asked the doctor and the medic.

The doctor mumbled something about Rylands, bullets and babies and strolled out. The medic went with him. And Gage turned to Lynette to get this show on the road.

"You're not leaving me," she blurted out. But then she shook her head. "I mean, you're not leaving me, are you?"

Gage hated that she'd spent one second worrying about that. He stood. Or rather tried to. But Lynette grabbed his good arm and had him sit on the examining table.

"I'm not leaving," he verified. "In fact, I'm not going back to the CIA. I'm staying here in Silver Creek. Maybe I'll even apply for a deputy job so I can spend more time with you and the baby."

Finally, he saw the relief on Lynette's face, and her breath just swooshed out. It was Gage's turn to catch on to her, and he eased her closer so that he had hold of her and she was standing between his legs. Since they were already halfway to a hug anyway, he pulled her even closer.

Yes, there was pain, but he didn't care.

Especially when he kissed her.

One taste of her mouth, and the last thing he felt was pain. Lynette did some floating, too, and made a silky little moan right before she melted against him.

"Your mouth can stir a lot of things inside me," she whispered. And then she did something amazing.

She smiled.

Her entire face lit up.

That put everything in his head and his body in their right places. Lynette was okay. His baby, too.

"I always thought you deserved better," he let her know, sliding his hand over her stomach.

"Then you should change your name to *better*, because you're what I want. What I've always wanted." Her breath broke on the last word, and tears watered her eyes.

He shook his head. "I have no idea why."

"Let me remind you." And she kissed the breath right out of him.

As reminders went, it was a darn good one. Even though Gage wasn't in any shape to drag her off to bed, he sure as heck could fantasize about it.

Later, he'd do more than fantasize.

She kissed him again and then stepped back. "You need that X-ray."

Gage didn't let her go. He snagged her hand. "I'm in love with you. You know that, right?"

More tears came, but she nodded. "I suspected as much. But it's good to have the words."

Then he would say them to her often. Daily, in fact.

"I'm in love with you, too," she added. "You know that, right?"

Now, it was his turn to feel the relief. "I suspected as much when you told me you hadn't had sex in ten years."

Gage kissed her again. "I think we need to make up for all that lost time."

She put her mouth against his ear. "I'll respect you in the morning."

He gave her his best devilish smile. "It's not respect I'm aiming for, darlin'."

Lynette laughed, and he realized it'd been way too long since he'd heard that. Another note.

Make her laugh daily.

"Will you marry me?" he asked.

"We're already married. Ten years now," Lynette reminded him.

Man, he had some anniversary gifts to make up for. He was ready to spend some serious time shopping and keeping Lynette happy.

"Then, marry me again?" Gage asked. "Go on a honeymoon with me so we can stay in bed for a week. Make that two," he corrected. "And we'll promise to love each other for the rest of our lives."

Her mouth hovered over his. "Deal."

Now, that was a word he'd wanted to hear. Gage hauled Lynette to him and he kissed her.

* * * * *

USA TODAY *bestselling author*
Delores Fossen's miniseries,
THE LAWMEN OF SILVER CREEK RANCH,
comes to a heart-stopping conclusion.
Look for Mason Ryland's story next month,
wherever Harlequin Intrigue books are sold!

REQUEST YOUR FREE BOOKS!
2 FREE NOVELS PLUS 2 FREE GIFTS!

♦ Harlequin®

INTRIGUE®

BREATHTAKING ROMANTIC SUSPENSE

YES! Please send me 2 FREE Harlequin Intrigue® novels and my 2 FREE gifts (gifts are worth about $10). After receiving them, if I don't wish to receive any more books, I can return the shipping statement marked "cancel." If I don't cancel, I will receive 6 brand-new novels every month and be billed just $4.49 per book in the U.S. or $5.24 per book in Canada. That's a saving of at least 14% off the cover price! It's quite a bargain! Shipping and handling is just 50¢ per book in the U.S. and 75¢ per book in Canada.* I understand that accepting the 2 free books and gifts places me under no obligation to buy anything. I can always return a shipment and cancel at any time. Even if I never buy another book, the two free books and gifts are mine to keep forever.

182/382 HDN FEQ2

Name	(PLEASE PRINT)	
Address		Apt. #
City	State/Prov.	Zip/Postal Code

Signature (if under 18, a parent or guardian must sign)

Mail to the **Reader Service:**
IN U.S.A.: P.O. Box 1867, Buffalo, NY 14240-1867
IN CANADA: P.O. Box 609, Fort Erie, Ontario L2A 5X3

Not valid for current subscribers to Harlequin Intrigue books.

**Are you a subscriber to Harlequin Intrigue books
and want to receive the larger-print edition?
Call 1-800-873-8635 or visit www.ReaderService.com.**

* Terms and prices subject to change without notice. Prices do not include applicable taxes. Sales tax applicable in N.Y. Canadian residents will be charged applicable taxes. Offer not valid in Quebec. This offer is limited to one order per household. All orders subject to credit approval. Credit or debit balances in a customer's account(s) may be offset by any other outstanding balance owed by or to the customer. Please allow 4 to 6 weeks for delivery. Offer available while quantities last.

Your Privacy—The Reader Service is committed to protecting your privacy. Our Privacy Policy is available online at www.ReaderService.com or upon request from the Reader Service.

We make a portion of our mailing list available to reputable third parties that offer products we believe may interest you. If you prefer that we not exchange your name with third parties, or if you wish to clarify or modify your communication preferences, please visit us at www.ReaderService.com/consumerschoice or write to us at Reader Service Preference Service, P.O. Box 9062, Buffalo, NY 14269. Include your complete name and address.

HI11B

Harlequin and Mills & Boon are joining forces in a global search for new authors.

In September 2012 we're launching our biggest contest yet—with the prize of being published by the world's leader in romance fiction!

Look for more information on our website, **www.soyouthinkyoucanwrite.com**

So you think you can write? Show us!

*In the newest continuity series from Harlequin®
Romantic Suspense, the worlds of the Coltons and their
Amish neighbors collide—with dramatic results.*

*Take a sneak peek at the first book, COLTON DESTINY
by Justine Davis, available September 2012.*

"**I**'m here to try and find your sister."

"I know this. But don't assume this will automatically ensure trust from all of us."

He was antagonizing her. Purposely.

Caleb realized it with a little jolt. While it was difficult for anyone in the community to turn to outsiders for help, they had all reluctantly agreed this was beyond their scope and that they would cooperate.

Including—in fact, especially—him.

"Then I will find these girls without your help," she said, sounding fierce.

Caleb appreciated her determination. He *wanted* that kind of determination in the search for Hannah. He attempted a fresh start.

"It is difficult for us—"

"What's difficult for me is to understand why anyone wouldn't pull out all the stops to save a child whose life could be in danger."

Caleb wasn't used to being interrupted. Annie would never have dreamed of it. But this woman was clearly nothing like his sweet, retiring Annie. She was sharp, forceful and very intense.

"I grew up just a couple of miles from here," she said. "And I always had the idea the Amish loved their kids just as we did."

"Of course we do."

"And yet you'll throw roadblocks in the way of the people best equipped to find your missing children?"

Caleb studied her for a long, silent moment. "You are very angry," he said.

"Of course I am."

"Anger is an...unproductive emotion."

She stared at him in turn then. "Oh, it can be very productive. Perhaps you could use a little."

"It is not our way."

"Is it your way to stand here and argue with me when your sister is among the missing?"

Caleb gave himself an internal shake. Despite her abrasiveness—well, when compared to Annie, anyway—he could not argue with her last point. And he wasn't at all sure why he'd found himself sparring with this woman. She was an Englishwoman, and what they said or did mattered nothing to him.

Except it had to matter now. For Hannah's sake.

*Don't miss any of the books in this exciting
new miniseries from Harlequin® Romantic Suspense,
starting in September 2012 and running
through December 2012.*

Harlequin®

SPECIAL EDITION

Life, Love and Family

NEW YORK TIMES BESTSELLING AUTHOR

KATHLEEN EAGLE

brings readers a story of a cowboy's return home

Ethan Wolf Track is a true cowboy—rugged,
wild and commitment-free. He's returned home to
South Dakota to rebuild his life, and he'll start by
competing in Mustang Sally's Wild Horse Training
Competition.... But TV reporter Bella Primeaux
is on the hunt for a different kind of prize,
and she'll do whatever it takes
to uncover the truth.

THE PRODIGAL COWBOY

Available September 2012 wherever books are sold!

www.Harlequin.com

HSE65691